Secrets

The Steamship Chronicles
Book One

Margaret McGaffey Fisk

TTO
PUBLISHING

Cover art and design by Margaret McGaffey Fisk

Cover Illustrations and Photography: The Ship "Favorite" Maneuvering Off Greenock, 1819 by Robert Salmon courtesy of the National Gallery of Art, Washington; Colin Fisk (photography); and Graechan (text graphics)

TTO Publishing logo design by Blue Harvest Creative
www.blueharvestcreative.com

Secrets

Copyright 2014 by Margaret McGaffey Fisk

This book is a work of fiction. The characters, incidents, and dialogue are drawn from the author's imagination and are not to be construed as real. Any resemblance to actual events or persons, living or dead, is entirely coincidental.

Published by
TTO Publications

ISBN-10: 1-63139-005-8
ISBN-13: 978-1-63139-005-0

First Print Edition

Visit the author at:
Website: www.margaretmcgaffeyfisk.com
Twitter: @Marfisk
Google Plus: +MargaretMcGaffeyFiskAuthor
Facebook: MargaretMcGaffeyFisk

Praise for the Books of Margaret McGaffey Fisk

Secrets

"Through her young heroine and hero, the author breathes life into a curious, exciting and often dangerous world of steam, sail, sentient machines, loyal friendships and deeds of quiet bravery undertaken in the face of widespread fear and bigotry, to deliver a clever, entertaining and unique new take on Victorian Steampunk."

— David Bridger, author of *A Flight of Thieves* (*Sky Ships*) —

Shafter

"Trina's life revolves around protecting her family and as a shafter, the lowest of Ceric society, her choices are limited to what she can steal. However, a chance at a new life aboard a colony-bound ship teaches her a new way of life and the price of unquestioned loyalty in this exciting tale, rich with cultural world building and science fiction adventure. This is a story you'll love, with a tale you won't want to see end!"

— Lazette Gifford, author of *Glory* —

"While the heroine yearns for another world, you'll crave any universe, any tale, created by this exciting new speculative fiction author. In Shafter, McGaffey Fisk delivers an interplanetary colony system and populates it with complex and sympathetic characters. Travel from the tunnels of Ceric to the stars beyond with a master thief and her master storyteller."

— Valerie Comer, author of *Majai's Fury* —

Other Works by
Margaret McGaffey Fisk

SEEDS AMONG THE STARS

(SCIENCE FICTION ADVENTURE)

Shafter

Trainee

The Captain's Chair (short story)

UNCOMMON LORDS AND LADIES

(SWEET REGENCY ROMANCES)

Beneath the Mask

A Country Masquerade

An Innocent Secret

THE STEAMSHIP CHRONICLES

(STEAMPUNK ADVENTURE)

Safe Haven (Prequel)

Threats

Gifts

Box Set 1 (Books 1-3)

SHORT STORIES (eBook only)

Forged

War Child

Curve of Her Claw (illustrated by Star Olsen)

Visit margaretmcgaffeyfisk.com for more information
about these and other titles.

1

S am had been working on one of her machines in the garden when her sister's maid came to collect her.

"Lady Stapleton calls for you," Kate said, looking at the machine with a narrowed gaze.

Abandoning her tools, Sam leapt to her feet and grinned, pausing only to give the machine a quick pat in farewell.

Lily and Henry had been gone for a full week this time. The winter's chills had taken a toll on her sister's health and so Henry delayed his business until she felt well enough to travel. He took Lily on his trips whenever he could, weather permitting, and her sister seemed happier for the time away from the worries of the estate.

Still, Sam missed them when they were gone.

"You walk proper now." the maid said sharply before Sam could burst into a run.

The woman seemed to have a sixth sense for when Sam might misbehave and took every opportunity to scold. She'd treated Sam like a feral child even before the maid's copper-link necklace got caught up in one of her bouts.

No matter how much Sam had tried to explain and apologize, the woman continued to glare whenever Lily and Henry could not see. She'd returned the necklace with its broken clasp repaired, but that made no difference. Even fixing the steam-powered heater so their piped water wouldn't freeze in the winter had failed to soften the maid's attitude.

It took all of Sam's focus to keep to a steady pace, but Kate's annoyance couldn't dampen Sam's growing excitement for all the maid schooled her walk.

"Now don't you be tiring your sister, Miss Samantha. She doesn't be needing any of your antics," the maid said when they came to a halt in front of the sitting room door.

Sam ignored the warning as she waited for Kate to sweep into the room first, a subtle breaking of tradition the woman used to put Sam in her place without drawing Lily's attention. But the maid only turned the silver knob, pulled the door open, and waved for her to enter.

Ducking her head to hide a cheeky smile, she stepped past Kate and into the room, anticipation wiping out the maid's unpleasantness.

"I'm so happy you're back." The words burst from her before she even looked around. "What did you find for me this time?"

Henry and Lily had gone to Dover, a full day's carriage ride from the estate. Lily always brought something back to make up for Sam's inability to leave, and ever since Henry set up a little workshop, those gifts often included small mechanical objects crafted by blacksmiths. Only the most complicated and well-used machines would make her lose control, and she so loved working with the devices.

Sam's gaze found the empty sofa with its elegant, carved wood legs, the table bare of anything, and finally, her sister on the stuffed armchair, looking even more frail than usual after her winter sickness. But color highlighted Lily's cheeks, streaks of red Sam knew meant a secret waiting to burst out.

She crossed to her sister and knelt before the chair, her lanky height taller than Lily's when seated. "What is it then? I know it's got to be something special with you all colored up."

Sam could hardly keep still as expectation triggered sparks of pleasure to dance along her nerves.

Lily still said nothing, the faint smile dropping from her expression. She put a hand on the top of Sam's red curls but did not move at first.

As always, her sister's presence brought with it calm enough to ease even the worst of Sam's episodes before something disastrous occurred. She leaned into the touch, enjoying the attention as Lily stroked her hair. But soon the quiet made her antsy.

"Hush, Samantha. Just sit a while."

If anything, the soft words made her more uncomfortable, especially with her sister's use of her full name.

Lily rarely did nothing.

She always had some work in her hands.

Sam had been growing steadily, and Lily often mended old clothes for the servants' children when she'd finished Sam's, one of the many reasons all of Henry's staff loved her. The table should have had her sister's latest project scattered across it, whether a crochet napkin or some clothing in need of repair.

Instead, it stood empty.

"I can't," Sam said after a pause. She pulled out from under her sister's hand and went to the sofa, folding her legs under her in a posture that usually made her sister scold.

Lily didn't even notice.

"It's a baby, isn't it? That's why you've been going to Dover with Henry, spending so much time away. That's what Cook says."

Sam refused to repeat Kate's speculations. Lily would never put a new child over Sam. They belonged together.

A faint smile touched Lily's mouth before she shook her head. "What have I told you about listening to the servant gossip?" As usual, the words held no heat. Lily understood better than anyone how much Sam craved company, even if it meant spending time in reach of the lady's maid and her barbs.

Her sister did not deny the gossip, but neither did she confirm it.

"That's not why I called you here, Samantha."

Tension rippled down Sam's back. Twice her sister called her Samantha when Lily knew she preferred Sam.

Lily twisted a strand of long blond hair between her fingers, looking anywhere but at Sam.

She tried to remember what she could have done to bring lines to Lily's face, but nothing came to mind. She'd even transformed a rusty old plow into a contraption to keep herself inside the workshop if she happened to feel a fever coming on while Lily was away. She didn't want her sister to have to worry.

"It's not about the plow, is it? Surely no one cared that I used it. Why the grass had grown up all around so I had to cut it free."

A laugh burst from Lily, leaving a comical expression in its wake as though her sister had not expected to find humor in the story. "You cut a plow free? And dragged it back to the workshop by yourself, I'd guess. It's not like Cook would have helped you...or Kate. Tell me you haven't co-opted one of Henry's workers? He needs them to keep the estate profitable, not running after your schemes."

Sam flushed and jerked her legs forward so they draped over the edge, her twisted skirt barely reaching her ankles and failing to hide the dirt-smeared feet below. "Old Mister Simmons is nice enough, especially after the steam-powered heater, but he keeps the others away from me."

Lily shook her head. "Maybe better one of them than on your own after all. Someday you may regret your boyish ways."

Sam sat straighter, hands pressing brocade on either side of her. "What's the point in being a lady? It's not as if anyone's going to come courting. They don't know I'm here. Nor will I have a coming out. Not even in the Merchanter Ball as you would have if Mother had lived. My prison's larger now, but it's not much different from that old barn. I can't leave, and no one comes to see me either."

She remembered Kate's admonishment a bit too late. Front teeth sank into her lower lip as she stared at Lily.

Sam had never spoken so in her whole life. She hadn't even known the continued strictures bothered her until right then.

Lily's pale features became drawn, and she half-rose from the chair as though coming to cuddle Sam like years before. "If things could have been different…"

Sam drew on the calm Lily's earlier touch had produced as she prepared to wash away the hurt in her sister's expression, but Lily never gave her the chance.

"That's actually why I called you here." Her sister settled back, shoulders curled with an invisible weight. "Do you remember how it was before Henry came for us? Do you remember our plans?"

"Safe haven." The words came out in a reverent whisper, too strong a dream for even Henry's generosity to squash.

Eight years had passed, but the memory of sitting on a pillow of moldy hay as Lily described what awaited on the Continent rose sharp as though yesterday. Lily had read accounts from their father's journals telling of a place where Naturals gathered without a care for who saw them transform a simple machine into the mechanical that lived at its heart. They spoke of a place where Sam would have friends, people around her who never once wore that look of fear her abilities brought forth. Even Cook, who had befriended Sam for her enthusiastic appetite, still kept a wary eye out for any sign of an approaching bout.

It had been a beautiful dream, something to keep a little girl warm at night as Lily worked herself almost to death earning their passage when they had only rumors to guide them after the crossing.

"But instead we came here." Her voice went flat when she'd intended to show Lily that she held no regrets.

In truth, most days the estate offered enough room to ramble and the workshop gave her the ability to play with her natural affinity to machines. If she didn't have many friends—only one really beyond her family—at least she didn't live in fear that her smallest slip would cost her everything, and worst, cost Lily. Only lately had disquiet rippled beneath the peace Sam had found here.

Kate's sour words had struck hard. Sure, neither Henry nor Lily showed any sign of resenting her presence, but neither had they filled the empty rooms with the children both had wanted. Now Sam had to wonder if the choice lay not in chance but in the same fear that hovered in the servants' eyes when they thought Henry couldn't see.

"Yes, we came here. And it's better for you than that old barn for sure, but wouldn't you want something more? You talk of Merchanter Balls, so I'd guess you've been haunting Henry's library again, but you can never have that here."

Lily rose, her skirts swirling down to tiny feet encased in slippers. "Wouldn't you prefer a place where you could follow your nature without restraint? Where you didn't have to watch your every instinct?"

Sam had never thought her sister unkind before.

She stared at Lily, mouth half open. "Of course I would," she said, jerking to her feet, "But it's not possible. It never was no matter how much we pretended. I try not to think on it."

A wistful smile crept across Lily's face. "I thought I'd taught you how important it is to have dreams. Sometimes that's all we have."

Anger melted away as Sam crossed to her older sister, noticing for the first time how they stood almost the same height despite more than ten years between them. "You did, and it's true. But we found our dream of a safe haven here, with your Henry and my workshop."

Lily shrugged and turned half away. "It's not enough. It never will be with you still trapped. You said so yourself."

Sam stared at her dirty feet, the earlier anger turned inward. "I didn't mean it," she said to her big toe. "I wasn't thinking."

A strangled laugh brought Sam's face up again.

"It's when we don't think that the truth comes out, and a surer truth I've never heard from your lips. Whether you admit to it or not, the confinement chafes. It has since you got over the delight of grass beneath your feet."

Sam crossed the toes of one foot over the other in a feeble attempt to hide the grass stains that always seemed present, wishing she'd stopped long enough to put on the slippers her sister preferred she wore.

Lily only shook her head. "You might have put the Continent from your mind, but I've had Henry make discrete inquiries since you turned thirteen. There's more to life than running wild in a cage. You deserve that as much as anyone, and the accounts in Father's journals prove there's something to find."

Sam barely heard anything past the fact that Henry had kept searching. The dream came back with the full force of longing, a vision of the two of them in true freedom now grown to include Henry's strength. "Has he discovered something?"

When Lily glanced away, Sam's shoulders slumped. There had been nothing despite Lily's hopes. She'd figured that out years ago, though she'd never let on.

Her sister straightened her spine. "He has found it."

The soft words took a moment to sink in. Tingling swept through her limbs, and her scalp tickled as the dream became reality.

Around her, the room broke into its component parts, metal highlighted in her vision. A mantelpiece clock she desperately ignored every day called out for mobility.

"You're old enough now to go on your own."

The rest of what Lily said hit with the force of a blow, silencing the aether-driven pull from the clock and everything else.

"My own? What of you and Henry? Why can't you come too?" Sam's voice spiraled up until it sounded much younger than her fifteen years, but she couldn't help the desperation in its tones. "We're supposed to be together."

The way Lily had avoided Sam's eyes now gained another meaning.

Her sister pressed both hands to her stomach and slumped into the chair. "We were supposed to be together, Samantha. Father asked me to keep you safe, and I have. But I can't give you what you need any longer. It's cruel to keep you here when I know there's a better place for you to be."

"Yes, a better place. But one with room for you as well. Like we'd always planned it." Sam grabbed Lily's fingers and laced them through hers. "Together."

Lily pulled free. "My place is here with Henry." Her voice trembled on the words.

Sam relaxed, sensing the weakness in her sister's argument. She had only to press, and Lily would give in. Her sister would let them stay together as they were meant to be. "Henry can come too. I'm sure there's a place for him on the Continent. Who wouldn't like your husband? It would be perfect." She reached for the hand again.

Lily pulled out of reach then raised her fingers to rub at her temple. "Henry belongs here. He has roots going back generations."

Sam stared at Lily. She couldn't believe her sister would even think such a thing, much less plan it.

Lily's expression didn't change. Her sister didn't laugh and reveal this to be a jest. The pain shining from her eyes showed the decision hadn't been lightly made, but made it had been.

"You really mean it. Just like Kate said." Sam took a step back toward the door. "You are going to cast me out. You have your normal life here with Henry, your trips to Dover, your hateful lady's maid. Why do you need a dangerous little sister who can never leave?"

She twisted and stumbled from the room, vision clouded with unshed tears.

Lily called her name, but Sam didn't stop. She couldn't.

2

S am longed for the comfort of her workshop. It was the one place she could be sure no one else would come to find her except Lily, and now she knew her sister wouldn't come either.

At the last moment, though, she sought refuge in her room, unwilling to chance a meeting with one of Henry's staff. She couldn't face questioning whether they'd been told she would be cast out, or whether they would rejoice when they learned of Lily's plan.

Her chest felt tight, as though she couldn't breathe, and her temples pounded out a rhythm nothing like the one signaling a bout of mechanical energy too strong to contain. No, this gaped more like a freshly dug well, too deep to see the bottom and too tall to climb out of should she tumble. She teetered on the edge of despair for the first time in her life, now when things were supposed to be better.

The room she'd once thought wonderful looked bare as she crossed the threshold and sank onto the bed, her eyes gone dry.

No clock rested on a shelf, no metalwork at all, and the furniture held only the simplest of contraptions. Her chest was just that, a lidded box rather than the drawers found even in the Cook's room. Every piece told her what she should have seen, her mind trapped in the knowledge that Lily had not denied Cook's theory.

The mechanical man she'd repaired back in London, and kept despite the dangers, came out to comfort her now. Her creations never denied her. They would trail after her, find her wherever she might go, if they could. They would never abandon her by choice.

Sam shoved it away.

Its chilled metal form held none of the comfort her sister had offered over the years. Before it could topple off the coverlet, though, she caught hold of its toothpick-thin arm and pulled it back against her chest. Her memory locked on the way Lily curved fingers around her womb when she thought Sam wouldn't notice, much like how Sam cradled her creation now.

The truth glared at her with the bright glimmer of fresh-beaten brass.

Lily was pregnant, but more, she didn't dare bring a child into a house where Sam, an unchecked Natural, roamed free.

All this time, in her workshop, or wandering across the fields and sending the cattle scattering with her latest invention, Sam had missed the obvious. She hadn't seen the choices in her furnishings, the way her workshop had bars inside and locks outside, nor in how no one knew she existed beyond servants loyal to Henry.

Lily loved Sam, but did not trust her, and she never had.

Sam folded both arms under her chin and stared out at the rolling green of Henry's estate. She longed for the peace she'd denied to her sister just hours before. Her gaze did not see the dog snapping at the heels of an early spring calf, or Mister Simmons calling the cattle boy to task.

What scrolled past her vision took the form of lecture after lecture as far back as she could remember. Lily telling her the same things over and over: to make sure they were safe, to make sure Sam stayed hidden, to make sure...

No matter how much she grew, no matter how much she read and learned, Sam would not be able to change her very nature. She could try all she liked, but never again to experience any emotion strong enough to trigger a bout, never to feel the pull of a metal object begging for a new form, seemed a greater curse than being trapped in a moldy stable. And no more possible than making an instrument capable of tearing away her ability to see the heart and soul of what others believed to be lifeless machines.

Awkward movement in the corner of her eye caught Sam's attention, and at first, she thought one of her contraptions had escaped. Then she saw it for the broken cart it was, a wooden one dragged by a farmhand. Her emotions had taken hold so strongly that she could see the soul in objects containing almost no metal, a rare event when aether clung best to metal in high concentrations. The nails holding it together should not have had any pull at all.

Where the farmhand cursed in words Lily would have blushed to hear, Sam saw possibility, a longing for this broken-down cart to be something different, something wonderful.

Her mechanical man twitched against her, no more comfortable with sitting still than she normally was.

Sam glanced from the cart to her creation and felt a bubble of laughter climb through her body where she thought joy lost to her forever.

"I don't have to go after all," she told the mechanical. "I just have to prove to my sister that I can help with her children. I can help them understand a bigger world than most can see, and I can be careful. Isn't my guard to lock me in the workshop proof enough of that? I can tell when a bout is coming and sequester myself."

The mechanical man offered no answer, speech not one of the abilities she'd found in the ethereal energy wrapped around its once-broken form. Much like the cart, she'd given it another chance to become something more and would continue to do so as long as it cried out for change.

"And if you can grow and change through the aether wrapped around your form, surely I can as well. The priests in Henry's books say we're born with a soul, that people are at least. So I must have more aether than you'll ever gather." Maybe someday she'd be able to go down to the village church and hear the priests on her own. That would prove to Lily she'd learned control. Not yet, but maybe someday. For now, it would be enough to show that she would never ever harm any child, much less one of Lily's.

She put aside her mechanical man with a peck on its little, geared cheek, and paused long enough to straighten her hair and skirt. When her bare feet met the woven fibers of the hall runner, Sam turned back to add stockings and slippers to her outfit. If she were to be a good aunt, she had to put her wild years behind her. Convincing Lily wouldn't be easy, but something as simple as shoes seemed a good start.

S AM'S RETURN TO THE SITTING room held none of the rush of her leaving. She contemplated all the ways she could help with children, from making a self-rocking cradle to entertaining them with mechanical men. There should be time to convince her sister while the baby grew inside Lily.

Her sister would forget about sending Sam away, and everything would be back to normal.

No. A smile crept over Sam's lips. It would be better than normal.

Fate watched over her because Sam ran into no one, not even Cook, before she reached the sitting room door. She must have left it ajar in her haste. A crack showed light from the windows beyond.

Sam paused, and in that moment, she heard the deep rumble of Henry's voice.

Good. Better for them both to hear at once. Then she wouldn't have to explain twice and chance messing things up.

Her palm touched wood, but before she could push the door open, Henry's words came through the slight gap.

"I'm capable of caring for both you and Sam. You know I am. This decision is tearing you apart, and I can't imagine Samantha's faring much better."

Sam couldn't move, unable to leave for all she knew it would be the right thing to do, and frozen stiff so she couldn't call out and reveal her presence either.

One muffled thud followed by another sounded as though Henry had dropped to his knees at Lily's side, much like Sam had done earlier. "I can't bear to see you hurting."

"Hush, Henry. You're not helping by taking my pain onto your own shoulders. The doctors don't know what's wrong. None of them—not a one—gave much hope."

Henry's groan muffled Sam's gasp as everything she'd thought true shifted.

Lily wasn't pregnant. Her sister was still sick—very sick.

"I don't care what they say. They're wrong. And so are you. You need Sam here. I can watch over her while you recover your strength. You just need more time."

Lily's voice sounded weak when she answered his refusal to hear her words. "You have to accept the truth, Henry. You've been nothing but devoted to Sam since you discovered her existence. No one could fault you for your care, even when something has gone wrong."

"Then why do this? Why hurt all three of us?"

Her voice hardened. "You think I haven't considered all the possibilities? You think I haven't tried to figure out a better answer? Samantha is trapped here. You should have heard her when I spoke of your discovery. It cut me that I'd kept it hidden for so long in the hopes something would change. Nothing changes. She won't get better any more than I will, and my pretending only cost her time she could have been happy among her own kind."

"She welcomes this?" His voice rose higher with each word, straining against his incredulity.

The strength went out of Lily's tones, and Sam had to lean forward to catch the end of her words.

"Until she learned she would go alone."

The door creaked where she leaned against it, and Sam held her breath, waiting for discovery. As much as she was afraid of what her sister would say, another scolding would be kinder than what she had heard.

Neither seemed to notice as Henry began speaking again, urging Lily to let go of this idea, to keep her family together as she'd always promised.

"Henry, stop. You're not helping as much as you want to. You know as well as I do that simple love is not enough for Sam. When her bouts come and she loses control, only my touch can calm her. What will you do once I'm gone?"

"You'll never be gone."

Lily sighed heavily enough for Sam to hear the exhalation of air. "You know that's not likely. And you can't afford to chance Sam running off and revealing her true nature. Neither can Sam. Do you know what Mister Simmons told me when we arrived? He was so proud of her. My lovely little sister has changed the workshop you made for her from a refuge into a prison. Do you know why? So she can make sure she doesn't cause trouble when a bout overcomes her. What kind of life is that for her? Sending her away is the only answer. Keeping her here is selfishness."

Sam wanted to burst through the door and protest, to say she didn't mind protecting them, but instead, she heard what lay behind her sister's words. She remembered how Lily's coughing lasted longer each year. The visits to Dover became something other than pleasure jaunts, her gifts less treats than an excuse.

Her sister lay dying, and rather than focusing on her own needs, she worried about Sam. Lily had always focused on Sam, and now she called herself selfish for keeping them together.

Samantha swore from that moment on she would do everything in her power to make this easier on Lily. If she could do nothing to help, at least she would no longer make things harder. It was time for her to stand on her own and prove Lily had raised her well.

Forcing her lips into a cheerful smile, Sam returned to her room to start packing. Lily needed rest, relief from the burdens she'd carried since she'd been a little younger than Sam was now.

If her sister had any chance of survival, Sam had to leave.

3

S am had all her things packed in almost no time at all. Most lived in her chest already. The biggest question lay in whether she could take any of her mechanicals. She suspected the answer would be no and mourned for their pain.

Her first mechanical man had come to her that way. Its Natural had vanished. Maybe he'd gone on to a safe haven, but Sam suspected a much different end to a Natural in the busy streets of London.

She settled down to wait for dinner, deciding it best to give Henry and her sister some time, but sitting still never came easy. Before she'd made a conscious decision to do so, Sam had the few tools she kept hidden in her room out again. Her adopted mechanical man would finish out his existence in this form, however long a mechanical lived. The least she could do was make one last fix. Though she couldn't see how he'd use the ability to spring up like a cricket locked in her workshop, he wanted this change.

The resonant chime of the dinner bell startled Sam. She glanced out the window to see the daylight already faded, time vanishing along with it. Dark never bothered her when transforming. The aether itself offered a glow strong enough to see by while it guided her through the change.

She jumped to her feet and wiped both hands down the sides of her skirt, wincing a moment later at the grease stains she'd left behind. Normally she wouldn't work in her room for that reason, but Lily deserved a rest before facing Sam again.

Sam blushed to remember her behavior. She'd acted like a petulant child. Lily never had the opportunity to behave so when she was younger, and Sam had given her no chance to explain. She suspected her sister would have kept the truth secret anyway, though.

The heat faded from Sam's cheeks as she contemplated how she would convince Lily and Henry. She set her mind to the dream and put aside the knowledge that she'd have to leave them here. For once, she needed to be the strong one. They must never suspect how much she feared facing the world outside on her own.

The others had already reached the table when Sam paused at the dining room archway.

Her sister looked exhausted.

Henry glanced up to see Sam first. "Ah, there you are," he said as though nothing had happened.

Sam realized he had no way to know that it had.

Lily's whole body tensed before she turned with a smile Sam could tell took more work than it warranted.

Sam focused on the dream a Natural safe haven represented so her smile held true emotion.

"Sit yourself down, Miss Samantha. Can't have the first course going cold now, can we?"

It took no effort at all to turn her grin on Cook.

Steam rose from the soup tureen, a fragrant mist unlike the output of the steam generators that powered the house and mill.

"Are you hungry?" Cook asked, her eyes twinkling as though she'd just come up with this joke instead of making it at every meal.

Sam lifted her bowl without a word, happy to accept not one but a full three ladles of the creamy orange dish.

A half-choked laugh came from Lily, drawing all their attention to the far end of the table.

Lily shrugged. "It's just I didn't expect you to have an appetite." The humor in her expression drained out as suddenly as it had appeared, leaving Lily pale with shadowed eyes.

Sam took a quick spoonful of the soup then replaced the utensil. "Why shouldn't I have an appetite? I'll need my energy for the trip to come. I can't imagine it'll be simple."

She waited for them to respond, either to her words or to the deliberately cheerful tone, but Henry and Lily only stared.

"I am still to go, am I not?" She knew full well they had no choice, but it was enough to break the shock.

"You want to go?"

That from Henry.

"Why wouldn't I? I've been dreaming of this for as far back as I can remember." She turned to her sister. "I'm sorry for my outburst earlier. It was a shock, and I'd always expected you to be with me." Another pause. "But it's past time I learn how to make shift on my own. You were taking care of me and supporting both of us when you were my age. I can manage a journey."

"You wouldn't start out alone."

"Lily, no." Henry put his hand over hers, but she pulled away.

"I will take you to the ship. I promise you, Samantha. This is for the best." Finally her smile seemed stronger and more genuine.

"I would like that." Sam's voice softened, but the emotion felt truer. With all that she now knew, to have Lily come with her even part of the way seemed a boon.

Henry frowned at Lily, but Sam understood his concern.

"I won't keep her long."

He swung his attention to Sam and shook his head. "I know you won't. And I will come too. It'll be a grand outing, one you deserve after all this time locked away on my estate. We'll need to make sure you have everything you require for the journey as well. Do you think you can hold fast for long enough to go shopping with your sister?"

A memory of the busy London streets, with machines racing along at every turn, swept over Sam. She stared at the soup that had, in fact, gone cold. "I'll do my best."

"You can have my hand the whole time, Samantha, and when you've had enough, Henry will finish getting what you need, won't you, Henry dear?"

He touched a napkin to his lips and set it aside, signaling an end to the course. "Yes, I can follow a list, but we'd best look at clothing and the like early in the day. I doubt Sam shares my measurements for all she's been sprouting up."

Sam and Lily both laughed at that, the image of Sam lost in Henry's clothes too comical to take without reaction.

Though Cook tsked when she saw Sam's poor effort on the soup, Sam made sure to do better on the other courses, her false willingness turned genuine. She never mentioned the packing that had ensured enough to keep her, nor her doubts about wandering a city of any size, even with Lily to cling to.

Everything would be perfect. She'd make sure of it.

*H*ENRY HAD EXPLAINED TO SAM how he needed a day to make final arrangements. He'd already spoken to various captains about securing a passage but had to discover which ships were in port. He also planned to draft letters of introduction, using his contacts to ease her path all the way to the Natural haven he had found.

A day seemed too long for Sam to maintain her delight, but soon she realized she had much to do beyond packing.

After breakfast, she wandered back to the kitchens, an act that drew a disgusted sniff from Kate. Somehow, the maid's attitude bothered her less with the knowledge that soon she would be well away from Kate's reach.

In a show of emotions that startled both of them, Sam threw her arms around Cook's robust form. "I'll miss you, Cook. Mealtime won't be the same without you laughing as you serve me extra."

The older woman pulled Sam against her flour-coated apron, neither caring about the mess.

Then Cook stepped back, her hands coming to rest on Sam's shoulders. "You're just worried you won't get enough to eat, though where you put it is anyone's guess."

Sam gave a quick headshake at the comment. "You're thinking of Lily again. My frame's broad enough to take what you dish out."

Cook blinked twice, her eyes glinting in the flickers of light from the flame-filled hearth. "You may be sturdy, but no one could call you stout, Miss Samantha. You pack away the food and then burn it just as fast. You be careful out there. Make sure you've always got enough to keep you, or you'll crisp up like a dry twig, you will."

"I can take care of myself. I swear I can. But no one will cook as well as you do."

Cook mussed Sam's tangled hair. "You always were a sweet-talker. How you get away with so much if you ask me. Just keep your mouth shut until you have your bearings. Too many will not take kindly to a precocious girl-child out in the wider world, especially those Continental folks. And don't you go trusting them either. They'll sell you a half-weight, all the while claiming it's worth twice a full pound."

Sam nodded, hearing the love in Cook's roughened voice better than if the woman had come out and said it.

"Now you go run along. I'm sure you've got more important things to do than hang out here with the likes of me. 'Sides, I've got the baking to take care of. You can't be setting out on a carriage journey with an empty belly. As like you'd eat the horses themselves."

Cook turned her back, but the dabs of flour at the corners of her eyes revealed the tears she'd tried to hide as much as Sam's blinking showed her own efforts to keep control.

"I'll miss you," Sam whispered a final time. She turned to run back through the servant hall to the main house before she could hear a response. She'd been so focused on losing Lily that she hadn't considered much about the rest of her life until now.

Everything would change, from the moment she woke in the morning to when she rested her head again on her pillow, and for a long time, it wouldn't be her pillow even, but rather some hostel or roadside inn.

She'd gone to Cook first because she thought it would be the easiest of her goodbyes, at least of those she planned to make. Instead, Cook made her realize what she'd be giving up.

Sam's feet dragged as she headed back to her room. In all the time she'd lived on Henry's estate, she had tucked little mechanical creations here or there so she'd always have one in easy reach should the need to transform come over her. She could ignore the cries of minor machines most of the time when an already transformed one lay within range, its soul more complicated and already growing.

But Henry had confirmed her fear the night before.

She would not be able to bring a single one of her creations on the journey. None could be trusted to know the truth about her. Instead, she'd travel as an orphaned cousin on her way to live with an aunt on the Continent. It would be better this way. With none to share in her secret, she had only herself to keep it hidden.

Visions of just how difficult that would prove to be led her to images of her mechanical creations flowing across the roads after her, of them swamping whatever ship Henry found for Sam, or worse, surging into the salty water and corroding as they tried to follow her across the ocean.

For the safety of those she left behind, Lily and Henry, Cook, even Kate for all she mattered only because of her connection to Lily, Sam had to make sure that didn't happen. They'd be accused of sheltering a Natural when the mechanicals were traced back to Henry's estate even if no Natural could be found.

More than just her creations were at risk.

Only that knowledge kept Sam going as she rounded up a simple pace keeper that had once been a letter opener, a small statue, and some twine from the fence around the estate. She paused outside the dining room to listen, but no one was within. In the back of a cabinet, she had tucked the tiniest mechanical man she'd made, from a lady's pocket watch that happened to get lost when Henry had received visitors. Another had been a bed warmer and now had a lead weight that ran through its coils.

One after another, she brought every stray mechanical back to the workshop, where even more lay, stood, or sat on shelves, tables, or the floor.

Some had the look of people, others even Sam didn't understand what they had wanted to be, but each held a tie to her, an invisible cord of aether that normally strengthened them both. She only hoped it would break if stretched too far, freeing them from the longing and freeing her from the same as well. Sam could make more mechanicals even if it didn't, but no Natural would appear on Henry's estate to lay claim to those she left behind.

Finally, Sam wheeled in the last freestanding mechanical.

She could not move those that were too heavy, or were like the steam-powered heater where she had transformed only a small portion of something much larger. But any she could gather now crowded the workshop, a place that had been more of a home to Sam than any other part of the estate.

Her cheek stung as salty tears dripped down past a scrape she hadn't noticed getting as she stretched and crawled into the spaces where she'd hidden her creations.

They could not speak. Most had too little aether to attain self-locomotion. Few were as sophisticated as the four mechanical men she'd made, counting neither the adopted one nor the mechanical she'd made for Henry from his grandfather's watch so long ago. Despite her hand in its creation, that one would follow no one but Henry and read the need to hide from his mind.

Though the mechanical men were the only creations that might understand her words, Sam passed between them all with soft murmurs and touches until she reached the door once again, her newest creation behind and to one side.

"I didn't build this for you, and I hope you'll forgive me for trapping you the way I've been trapped, but I can't chance you coming after me. You won't be able to without destroying yourselves and everyone I care for on the way."

None of them showed any reaction to her words, but she thought she heard a moan as she stepped through the door and triggered a lock only she could open. The noise could have come from the springs as they dropped a crossbar into place then shoved bolts in to make the contraption fast. It could have been the wind through the rafters of the work-shop.

Sam didn't think so, and the thuds against the solid oak door a moment later proved her right.

She put both hands to the rough wood, pressing hard enough to feel the grain. "I'm sorry."

They wouldn't be able to hear her over the surge of noise beyond. They'd never know what it cost her to lock them away.

Sam knew, and it took all her strength not to trigger the mechanism to open once again so she could climb in there with them.

4

S am woke just before dawn, her stomach full of knots.

She swung both legs out of bed, untwisted her nightgown, and went to the window.

Last night, she'd gone to sleep at peace with the decision to go. She'd said her farewells and had started looking forward to the journey and to the dream of others like herself.

Now, though, she couldn't settle.

Then Sam heard the sound that had jolted her from her rest—coughing.

She made it half way to the door before remembering she wasn't supposed to know how sick Lily was. If her sister found out, Lily would doubt Sam's reasons for agreeing to go and waste energy she desperately needed worrying about Sam instead.

Waiting there in her room took all the strength Sam could muster with little left to keep the urges in check. Her fingers itched to transform, but she'd removed anything she could have used to distract herself.

Sam could only sit on her bed or stare out the window, trying as hard as she could not to strain for the sound of any more coughs.

The sun finally rose high enough for Sam to dress and comb her hair into some semblance of order before running down the stairs to breakfast in as good an imitation of her normal self as she could manage.

The breakfast room stood empty.

No food steamed on the sideboard, and neither Henry nor Lily sat at the table waiting for her. They always arrived before her. Sam made sure of it by waiting that extra little bit each day, but she'd failed this morning. Shaken, she pulled out her chair and sat down, hands folded in her lap.

Henry arrived soon after, his cravat undone and his hair still mussed. He offered a smile, but Sam could tell it wasn't genuine.

"We're on our own this morning, Sam. Cook received word earlier that her sister's labor has started. Family comes first."

An awkward pause followed his words, but Sam broke it with a sigh. "So no hot breakfast? Or is Lily off making something."

She'd tried to brush past the unspoken knowledge that they were breaking family rules by sending her away, but Henry's expression tightened more instead of relaxing.

Another pause then Henry said, "Lily's lying in. She was up last night working on something or other and tired herself beyond measure." His words would have been casual if not for the strained tone and the lines on his face.

Sam fought the need to press for answers. She knew he hadn't told the truth even without his expression to give him away. Though she'd tried not to listen, the coughing that had woken her continued for some time before it eased.

"Well," she said with as bright a smile as she knew how to make, "I'll just cook something myself."

The look on Henry's face would have been laughable if that very fear wasn't taking her life away.

"No, don't trouble yourself," he said in a rush. "Kate's putting something together."

Sam failed to hide her expression before he saw it, no better at stilling her features than he was.

"I know the two of you don't get along, but she's a decent hand with a toasting flat. And Cook made some lovely rolls and pastries for our trip."

Both of them glanced toward the door.

Lily did not appear, no matter how much they wanted her to.

Instead, Kate came through with a smile for Henry and a scowl for Sam, her hands occupied by a platter piled high with the pastries Cook had been making the day before.

"I thought those were for the trip."

Henry shook his head at her, but Kate ignored Sam's comment as though she hadn't spoken.

Sam stuck her tongue out at Kate's back, earning a choked laugh from Henry.

Here was a person Sam wouldn't miss one bit. Kate couldn't fall behind Sam fast enough, in her opinion.

Henry's eyes sparkled with barely suppressed humor despite his attempt to give her a stern look. The break from worry had been good for both of them, and yet it reminded Sam this would be her last breakfast at the estate.

"When do you think we'll be leaving?" she asked, trying to focus on the positive.

He glanced at the door again and his brow furrowed. "When your sister is ready. It shouldn't be too long."

Sam tried to be patient.

She kept herself from the workshop to avoid upsetting her mechanicals further. She even played a few notes on the grand piano, but had to walk away when the little screws holding each string in place started giving her ideas. Lily's sitting room called to her, or rather the mantel clock did, but Sam refused to give in to the pull.

The kitchen held no interest with Kate presiding, and her bedroom seemed even emptier than usual with her things packed away.

After struggling with the house as long as she could, Sam wandered outside, but she soon found her feet pointed toward the workshop when she'd meant to go to the nearest field.

Henry had retired to his study some time ago. Maybe she'd waited long enough to check with him.

When she reached his room, the door was ajar, giving hope that Lily had come down.

Instead, peeking in, she could see Henry, his head resting on both arms.

She started to turn away, but he raised his head at the slight noise of her shoes against the wood floor. Had she not dressed for the trip, she would have made a better escape.

"You've come to see when we're leaving."

His voice came out flat, exhausted.

Sam shrugged. "I guess we're not leaving today? I don't need anything more than I already have."

Henry gave her a weary smile. "Your sister is still sleeping. I've sent a runner to borrow a steam carriage one of our neighbors recently purchased. Lily will be better rested tomorrow. We can still see you aboard your ship."

"That sounds grand." She said nothing more, torn between excitement at riding in a contraption she'd only heard Lily describe once when they still lived in London and the fear that she wouldn't be able to keep herself under control with such temptation within reach.

Once she attained the relative safety of the hallway out of Henry's hearing, Sam whispered to herself, "Lily will be there. Lily will help keep me calm."

Her hands settled against her sides, no longer twitching in anticipation of a complicated working.

If only Lily could calm Sam's fears for her sister as easily. Lily only needed to sweep down the stairs, laughing at herself for having overslept. Then everything would be all right.

Sam looked to the stair, wishing she still thought Lily pregnant even if that meant believing her sister would cast her aside in favor of a child.

Lily didn't appear, nor did Sam's worries lessen, but she'd promised herself that she would not make things worse for her sister, and by extension, for Henry. She wouldn't question or complain. All this had to happen whatever she thought about it, and she wouldn't be the one to make it harder.

5

Nat put his pencil down, clamping it within the slot he'd helped the ship's carpenter build into the captain's desk. "All done with my paper, Captain Professor, sir."

"You needn't be so eager, Nat, my boy. Your parents put you in my hands for a reason, and that had little to do with my sailing skills." The captain crossed to the desk from his bed and lifted Nat's paper to catch the dim light coming in the window.

Nat leapt up in time to grab the captain's arm and steady him against the lurch of their vessel, the Channel still rough after a recent storm.

"Would you look at this, boy? It's a disgrace. You haven't a lick of learning in you. Even your script is hasty and poorly drawn. Your thoughts are all on rigging when they should be on the world."

The lecture he'd heard many times poured over Nat's head. He understood how the professor felt about being ripped from his university seat, but Nat could find nothing wrong in wanting people to work for a living. He had no quarrel with learning a trade, especially when it meant captaining a ship. The captain had everything Nat had ever wanted, and no interest in the work at all.

Captain Paderwatch gave him a gentle cuff about the ear, nothing like the schooling Dennis Trupt, the first mate, would have managed. "You're not listening to a word I say, are you,

Nat? You're no different than those fools who think closing the universities will somehow make the world better. Sure, it's easy to see productivity as work of the hands, but easy doesn't make it true. Mark my words, boy, it's the work of the mind that's needed to take us to the next step. Look at how they handle Naturals. Inhumane it is. Locking them up like that because they can do something no one else can. If the science academies still existed, we could study those poor souls and discover just how it is they transform basic machinery into something more. A waste throwing all that possibility away."

Nat nodded in time to the captain's words, but contributed nothing of his own to the conversation. He'd long learned the captain would eventually run out of steam, and he was a good master. Even the career sailors liked the man, in part because Captain Paderwatch did not see fit to interfere in what he didn't understand. They were grateful for the captain's skills in navigation, and his book learning and extensive travels before the age of industry dawned had come in handy a time or two.

It didn't harm Nat's position with the crew either that he took the brunt of the captain's need to educate. The others saw it as a sacrifice on their behalf, and Nat was happy to make it as long as they offered their own brand of teaching once the captain tired of battering Nat's brain with facts and philosophies he'd never have need of.

"Oh, get on with you, boy. I'm sure Mister Trupt can find something for you to do more to your liking."

Nat didn't require a second telling as he crossed to the door as fast as politeness allowed.

He didn't move fast enough, though, as the captain caught his arm before he could step through.

"I expect you back after supper for some more chart work."

"Yes, sir!" Nat needed no effort to put enthusiasm in his voice at this command. A paper on the marriage practices of some obscure people the captain met in his voyages held no value Nat could see, but a captain required skills in navigation, and Nat fully intended to reach that stature someday.

MISTER TRUPT, THE CAPTAIN PUTS me in your hands," Nat announced, planting his feet as the first mate had taught him.

The man might look like he just stepped out of a bare-fisted boxing ring, complete with a poorly healed break in his nose and a scar that marred one cheek, but he'd been nothing but straight with Nat.

They shared a lopsided grin before Trupt sobered. "Get yourself on the rigging and check those sails for storm damage. The last thing we need is the Company taking from our pay to cover repairs another time."

Though Nat hated thrusting a stiff bone needle through the heavy canvas, the cut in pay hurt him as well, if less than those with family on shore to feed. They used the sails more than the East India Trading Company wanted to admit, the massive steam engine an early model that offered less speed than a stiff wind. At least the smokestack had been upgraded to the latest filtration system once they realized the coal dust and occasional sparks proved hazardous to the sails. Not that the Company cared for their safety, but repairs meant dock time when the ship earned nothing.

Nat glanced toward the hatch that led down to the engine room, his mind lost in the possibilities if Mister Garth would only let him near the engine. Not that Nat had any special training in steam engines, mind you. He knew nothing more than any other member of the crew.

But he wanted to learn every aspect of the ship, especially the mechanism that drove their protected paddles, and Garth's gruff refusal bothered him.

The first mate caught his head and turned it back to face the rigging. "Keep your mind on the task at hand, boy, and you'll go far. Keep looking for the next one, and you'll trip over your own feet in the process."

Nat flushed as he headed off to join the others already up the ropes. He'd been foolish enough to tell Trupt his dream of becoming a captain when he'd been aboard not even two days. Instead of laughing, though, the first mate encouraged him at every turn, gently, or not so gently, schooling him when he drifted off his goal. Nothing meant more than when, a few weeks earlier, Trupt had said, "If you keep going as you are, you'll surely make captain in my lifetime."

Lost in thought, Nat tripped over a coil of rope and ran head first into the pins right below the rigging he'd been aiming for.

Phil, one of the riggers with an uncanny balance on the ropes, flipped upside down to give him a steadying hand. "You've spent too much time locked in that cabin. Forgot your sea legs, you have. Wandering around the deck like a drunkard."

One of the others barked a laugh. "Our cabin boy's from the same stock as the captain. He's still green behind the ears and never tossed back enough to make him stagger."

Phil waited for Nat to join him, and together they scampered up to the others, Nat taking extra care to watch how Phil placed his feet and levered his rail-thin body so that he walked the ropes as though on dry land.

"Don't you let their teasing get you red," Phil told him. "When we finally limp into port, I'll show you the real sailor's life. You should know what it's truly like, if you know what I mean."

This time Nat flushed bright red all the way to the tips of his ears if the rush of heat meant anything. At least his over-grown hair, curling down past his collar, kept some of his embarrassment hidden.

"You're scaring the boy," a third rigger called with a laugh. "He's not ready to meet that side of the universe, not the drinking or the other manly entertainments."

Nat knew better than to let their teasing get to him. He offered a lopsided grin in return. They spoke only the truth. His upbringing had been sheltered compared to theirs, and some-day he'd do something about that, but not with Phil in the lead. If the man weren't the best rigger any ship could claim, he'd have been kicked ashore to find his own way back from any one of the many ports he'd had to be carried in from.

After twisting his knees in a space of rope and wrapping one hand securely, Nat leaned out to check what looked to be a loose thread on the sailcloth. Even something as tiny as a dangling end could become a major tear under the force of a full wind.

But though he squinted to improve his view, he couldn't be sure if what he saw was thread or shadow. The first mate would cuff him hard if he called for the sail to come down and it turned out to be a shadow. Phil might have been joking about showing Nat the seedier side of the next port, but he'd been right on about the limping. Storm winds were unreliable, but even now they had the sails storm-rigged in the hopes of getting an extra jump over that offered by the old steamer.

The sailors liked to call it a teakettle, but only when Kyle Garth was out of hearing. No one wanted to be on his bad side. The worst task a man could be given was feeding the boiler. The heat from the open flame made them sweat even when snowflakes drifted across the deck and any better-earning vessel would have already stowed for the winter or not yet freed rather than chance ice floes.

But the engineer wouldn't even let Nat take that task, though he couldn't for the life of him figure out what he'd done to offend the man.

Nat forced his attention back to his current duty.

Mulling over his failure where the engineer was concerned did no good, and whatever he might think about the steam engine, Nat couldn't argue the importance of the sails even had he wanted to. With a gulp of air, he pried his fingers loose. He channeled Phil, determined to prove he could conquer the task, and let go, his legs the only hold as he swayed toward the sail to get a better look.

A high-pitched whine cut through the wind and waves to pierce his ears at that very moment.

The whole vessel lurched, a ripple of blocked movement sending creaks and groans from one end to the next. The strain translated into jerking of the rigging a heartbeat later, not late enough for Nat to have time to secure his position, though.

The ropes he'd twisted around his knees seemed to vanish from around him.

He started slipping. His head flipped downward, and he could see the hard wood deck approaching at a speed having little to do with safety.

Just when he'd given up hope, his ankle caught, wrenching muscle and maybe bone as he jolted to a stop, the wood grains no more than a body length below him.

A string of curses strong enough to turn the air around Mister Trupt a cloudy blue reached Nat's ears, with enough mixed in to reveal the cause of the strain, though there'd been little doubt.

The steam engine had seized again, its gears locking the paddles in place so the water became a wall to block their progress.

Some days the engine seemed more trouble than a help, but at least the distraction meant no one had been paying attention to his own undignified predicament.

Nat twisted around, biting his lip to keep a cry of pain from gaining voice as he tried to pull himself up.

A hand caught hold of his before he could reach the ropes above him and jerked Nat the rest of the way.

He choked on a scream, only to realize the pain in his ankle had lessened rather than growing.

Phil grinned down at him. "Never worth chancing an ankle. Can't climb the ropes without one of them. Take care in your scrambling."

And with that warning, Phil raced off to check another part of the rigging for damage, either of the wood supports or the rope itself.

Nat hung there, relieved to be upright as reaction settled in. He'd come so close to losing all goals and dreams, to ending his very life. His limbs trembled, and only the grip at four separate points kept him on the ropes.

Unable to do anything else, Nat tried to distract himself by staring out across the sea, the unrelieved waters soothing in comparison to his fears.

What he saw made no sense at first, and then it did.

That strip of brown against the horizon meant they finally neared the port they'd been heading for, a full day late thanks to storm winds on a different tack and their engine's quirks.

"Land ho!"

His shout was lost beneath the curses and commands as the crew identified new damage they'd have to report to the Company or repair out of their own pockets, either choice often amounting to the same thing.

Nat jerked his tangled foot clear, gingerly placing it in a different join. The ankle ached but held, so he scrambled the rest of the way to the deck, waiting until the last moment to jump clear.

"Land ho," he shouted again, run-jumping his way to the first mate.

Mister Trupt caught him by the shoulder. "You need to see the ship surgeon?"

Nate shook his head, knowing it best to avoid the surgeon unless the choice meant sure death. "I'm fine. It's twisted a little, but as soon as I wrap the ankle, it'll hold."

"Good. Get your wrapping done, then lend a hand."

He'd already turned away to address the next crisis, but Nat called him back. "Mister Trupt, that's not why I came for you. Look." Nat pointed toward the shadow of land, less visible from the deck with the spent storm still sending ripples through the water taller than a man's height.

Trupt raised a hand to shade his eyes and stared, willing enough to give credence to Nat's observation. The decision was rewarded as, a short time later, his eyes narrowed when he saw the same as Nat had seen. "Land. Maybe we'll survive this voyage after all." His words sounded bitter, but he spoke them with humor lacing his tone.

The first mate slapped Nat hard enough on the back to send him reeling. Trupt steadied him and grinned. "You've a good set of eyes, boy. Maybe we should send you to the crow's nest for a spell."

Nat glanced up to the very top of the main mast, unable to stop his shiver.

"Or maybe that's not a reward you're seeking just now. You were up in the ropes when that cursed engine seized, weren't you? I can see how that would put the fear in a man. Just don't let it catch hold of you or you'll never shake the bite."

He turned away, the conversation clearly over. With land in view, the first mate had even more to do than assess the damage.

Nat limped off to his hammock to find a scarf or shred of an old shirt he could use to bind his ankle. There were sails to check, and he took Mister Trupt's advice as pure gold. The riggings would not lay claim to him, nor would they hold him back.

6

Though he'd seen shore early in the day, the winds were against them. Garth got the steam engine moving again, but it did little to speed their passage. Still each of the sailors worked to prepare for landing in their own way, confident they'd soon make dock.

This time Nat had been assigned to Jenson, the ship's cook.

"Would you take a gander at this list himself gave to me?" Jenson said, waving the same paper that had brought Nat down to the kitchen in the first place. "Cucumbers, sweet jellies? What does he think this is? Some mansion house?"

Nat smiled and nodded in the right places, unwilling to admit he'd grown up on the same fare the captain demanded for his table. At least Captain Paderwatch could afford the luxuries he wanted, though they'd become hard to find in the ports their ship was sent to. This only made the list longer whenever they landed on their native soil.

Jenson squinted in the weak light seeping in through a shaded porthole. "There's not a bit of good stew and potato on this list. The captain will blow away on this feeding. It's not like he has much skin on his bones to speak of."

A laugh he failed to stifle escaped at that grumble. Jenson's words held a little too much truth for Nat to keep silent. The captain cut a slender figure if one was being kind and had the look of a scarecrow when the sailors spoke of it hunkered down against a storm.

Guilt drove him to his feet from where he'd been peeling the very potatoes Jenson so loved. "The professor wasn't meant for this life. Why, he's seen more of the world than I bet you know exists, and all that before he reached a mature age. You should hear him tell of the far flung island cultures he's studied."

Jenson shrugged. "I didn't mean anything by it, young Nat. He's a good man at heart when many don't give that much. Still, ain't any use for that kind of learning, book or 'scientific expeditions,' as the captain calls them, in the real world."

Nat winced to hear the cook butcher Professor Paderwatch's common phrase, but this time his laughter held no guilt at all, against the captain at least. "Jenson, you're wrong about that. We're the slowest of the steam vessels. As unreliable as a pure sail ship with the hull of the most ungainly tugboat to hear the crew speak of it. Just how do you think your share is so decent?" He might complain about the papers, but the knowledge behind them offered insights other captains didn't share.

"I'm thinking our Mister Trupt has much to do with that."

Jenson's statement left no room for debate, and yet Nat couldn't let it stand.

"The captain knows just what people need and where to get it no matter what port the Company sends us to. He uses his share of the hold on goods that can cover our expenses. I've seen him do the calculations. Even helped him out a time or two. He might not know much about sailing, but what he does know keeps all of us fat and happy. Even Mister Trupt would say so."

"Now don't you get so riled up, especially with that peeling knife still in your hand."

Nat flushed as he realized he'd been waving his knife about with little thought to the consequences if the engine should balk another time, as it had twice already since dawn.

"But…" The cook slapped the captain's list on the table. "Maybe he does deserve some of these strange victuals after all. I'm not much with the calculating, beyond the weight of flour we'll need for how many months at sea. If you say he's doing us right, you'd be in a better place what with all the time you spend in his cabin with those musty books of his. He's a good man, I'll give you that much. I'm just glad we have Trupt to sail the ship. The captain would have to use all those fancy tongues he claims if he had charge of the wheel. He'd have us aground in foreign lands on every voyage with that contraption he swears by. At least the risk of steering us wrong is slight, what with it rarely doing much of anything."

Nate gave a grunt of agreement and turned back to his task, the potatoes slippery and his fingers rough from layers of starch. Captain Paderwatch had found the navigation tool on one of their passages, but it didn't seem to read the charts the same way the captain had been teaching Nat to, when it functioned at all. Still, something about complicated machines drew the former professor like a Spaniard after gold. From the clutter in his cabin, this love had started before even the drive of industry did away with higher learning.

"Don't you scrape them too close to the bone, boy. Peelings might taste a little better with some innards on them, but those thin slices of white, well they won't do naught but melt away on their own."

Nat glanced at the potato in his hand to see he'd been slicing the same side over and over until translucent white strips lay among the darker skins. "Sorry," he muttered.

Jenson only laughed. "Good thing we're heading to port to restock. Those'll be the last of the bin. If you hadn't caught sight of land, the waste'd be criminal. Yon captain might keep us well off, but not even he can control the winds, or that crazy contraption Kyle Garth likes so much. You're right she's slow. Why I could tell you of some of the crews I've fed on vessels that swept the Channel under them like a milkmaid cleaning out the old hay. Used to be more to the merchant life than just chugging along slower than a walking pace if only we could walk on water."

Settling onto his stool a little more comfortably, Nat kept to the task at hand while he listened to Jenson tell of other ships and other voyages. Half of the tales were sure to be false, but with enough truth in them to feel grand in the telling. Better this than another arithmetic lesson, and at least Jenson didn't scowl when Nat's thoughts drifted.

Nat held no ill will for the light scolding over the potatoes. He'd earn his passage and suffer his punishments well enough, knowing them to be earned just as much.

7

hat evening, Nat sat down to a meal of hearty beef stew, the results of his own labors in some small part. A half dissolved white strip of potato lay across the top of his serving, a deliberate gift from Jenson he could be sure.

The crew treated him much as they would any of their own—teasing and chastising went hand in hand with stiffer punishments and greater rewards. If not for the time in the captain's cabin, they might forget he came from the same kind of polished background as Captain Paderwatch. Nat made sure he worked as hard as any of them.

"It might not be the fare you've come to expect when you share my table, Nathaniel, but eat up. It'll be a busy day tomorrow when we reach Dover. There's much to do and little time to do it in if we're to have any chance of keeping to our schedule."

Nat swallowed his smile and dug into the stew with an enthusiasm his dinner partner obviously did not share. At the last moment, he remembered to tear off a chunk of bread and dip it at the end of his fork, something unnecessary, and inappropriate, when he ate among the crew.

The captain nodded in approval, but his own bread lay untouched, his mind clearly on something else.

"Everything all right?" There was a risk in asking, but better to chance a lecture on some far-off island where no one in their right mind would go than let the captain run with an idea. Captain Paderwatch was likely to propose the most out-landish things left to his own devices, one of the reasons few among the crew resented Nat's extra privileges. Meals in the captain's cabin meant as much time spent turning the captain aside from trouble as eating richer victuals most of the crew would not appreciate any more than Jenson did.

Captain Paderwatch tapped his bread on the table, dislodg-ing a few weevils, but still didn't tear any off. "You're getting along all right, aren't you, Nathaniel? If you'd rather try your hand at another trade, or even seek position on a better-equipped vessel, there's no harm done. I won't hold it against you."

Nat started shaking his head before the captain got halfway into this speech. "No, sir, I'm happy here, sir. Don't send me off. If I'm doing something wrong, just tell me. I know I don't always focus like I should, but I can try harder—"

His rapid speech broke off when tears of laughter rolled down the captain's fine-cut cheeks.

"I have no problems with your efforts, Nat," the captain said after regaining control, using the nickname the crew pre-ferred. "The opposite if anything. The men seem to have tak-en to you well enough, and you do good work. It can get frus-trating, though, with a ship like this one. I've heard the men talk. I can't help them, but your mother made me responsible for you."

Nat couldn't have been more surprised had a whale leapt on board just then and asked for passage. Here he'd been right with the crew in thinking the captain paid little attention to the goings on of the ship when he should have known better. A professor used to observation could not help but notice the life aboard their small ship.

"They know it's not your fault," he blurted. "They like you."

The captain shook his head. "Oh, I'm sure they tolerate me well enough. Not like any of us have a choice in the matter. But it's you I was asking about. I want to be able to give a good report to your mother, who just might take it upon herself to journey down to Dover for a sight of her boy." He stopped talking to stare at the ceiling for a long while before frowning. "Though I suppose that can't happen since I'll be posting a letter to her when we land, and we're not staying longer than it takes to resupply and get our orders." He shrugged. "No matter. I still need to know what to tell her."

Nat gave a genuine smile as he said, "Mister Trupt seems to like me, and the men don't tease me more than is to be expected."

"And what of Mister Garth? You expressed an interest in the steam engine when you first came aboard, did you not?"

With the threat of a letter to his mother looming, Nat thought discretion might serve him better than a complaint against the grumpy engineer. "I haven't had much time for that yet, Captain. Mister Trupt says I have much to learn."

"Ah, Mister Trupt. He would say something like that and expect you to apprentice for a year per task or some such strict ruling. Now there's a true sailor in the old style. He used to be on wind vessels, don't you know? And weren't those the days. At the wind's will and with no knowledge of where we'd end up. Drifting across the world itself to discover what lay on the other side. Now I was never the first to go, mind you, nor did I venture as far from civilization as some are attempting, but still, the people could be so different you'd never imagine we were the same species. Some still doubt that to be the case, but I say you must look beyond the skin and see what makes us brothers."

The captain's probing had come to an end. Nat settled in for a very different experience than when he listened to Jenson or the other sailors. Between one breath and the next, a story became a lecture, teaching him all about places he'd never go because the people Professor Paderwatch so adored had little to trade and even less interest in what the civilized world could offer.

His blessing came in the late hour, because not far into another grand teaching, a yawn broke through the captain's speech.

"Well now, that's enough for one night. We should reach land early tomorrow, and there's much to be done...as I already said, didn't I? Go on with you. I'm for my bunk and you should be too."

Nat didn't wait for a second command. He slipped out the door and headed for his hammock, the captain's lectures better even than a sleeping drought for putting the head down and sending it off into dreamland.

8

Henry came for Sam before the sun rose the next day, but she was already dressed.

Strain drew lines in his face, and she feared the worst, but he offered a weak smile. "Lily's up and about today, preparing for the trip. If we leave now, there might be time to go for a little shopping before your ship sails at noon. With the steam carriage, it's only a few hours from here, or so the coachman tells me.

He paused to share a moment of delight at the amazing speed, a connection with Sam that had only grown since the time she transformed his grandfather's watch into a mechanical man.

Any other would have been horrified. Not Henry.

The grin her thought provoked soon faded, and Sam turned away, unwilling to let him see the loneliness on her face. She had only a little while before they would be off, and then a few short hours before leaving them behind forever. Surely she could keep her mourning to herself.

They headed downstairs for a quick breakfast composed of the last of Cook's pastries. The cook was still off helping her own family, and Kate showed little ability and less inclination.

Lily didn't come down to eat, taking a tray in her room instead.

"This is hard for her," Henry said. "She wants what's best for you, but she'll miss you horribly."

Sam agreed in silence, hearing the part he didn't say as much as what he did.

Lily stayed up there to conserve her strength before doing one last act for Sam. Only once the ship sailed would Lily give herself permission to rest and heal. Her sister had always been that way, making sure everyone and everything else was taken care of before looking to herself.

In no time at all, Henry and Sam stood on the circular driveway with her trunk and one other left empty in anticipation of the purchases still to be made.

The coachman seemed nice as he handed her belongings up to the luggage rack on the roof. "A grand adventure for a young lady. Preparing for your coming out, are you?"

"Something like that," Henry said, stepping in to the rescue.

The coachman had as little to do with proper position as Cook, though whether that came from the equipage he drove or his cheerful nature she had no way to know.

Sam took an instant liking to him, especially when, once the luggage was stowed, he took Henry on a tour of his vehicle and did not comment as she tagged along.

"It has an elaborate suspension system to compensate for the roughness of the road at such speeds, and you'll notice the iron on the wheels is extra thick. I suspect we'll be replacing that a time or two in the coming months. I've a spare wheel in the back should we run into trouble unexpectedly."

Sam joined Henry in admiring the craftsmanship, but all the while she could feel the generator and engine within. It lay as though sleeping, aether gathered around like a pillow over its workings.

"Shouldn't we be going?"

Lily's arrival, late as it might be, offered a welcome distraction. Sam counted on her sister's presence to keep the siren call of the mechanism quiet.

Henry rushed up the entryway steps to help his wife down. Once she moved into the light, though, Sam could see just how pale and shaky Lily appeared.

She rushed to take her sister's other side, ignoring a feeble hand wave intended to dissuade her.

But before Sam could reach Lily, her sister stumbled.

Henry held on as best he could, but still Lily sank to the stone steps, sweat glistening on her forehead and cheeks despite a layer of powder.

"I'm fine. We have to go."

Sam had to lean in to hear her sister's words. She sent a stricken look to Henry. How could she pretend not to notice this?

"Help me with her," Henry said, his voice deeper even than usual. "We need to get Lily back inside."

This time her sister didn't protest.

Sam hoped she recognized the futility rather than lacked the strength.

With Lily stretched out on the sofa in the receiving room, Henry looked to the clock, winced, and declared, "We need to go now."

Sam balked, a scowl settling over her features. "You're not leaving Lily like this, are you?" She remembered her decision to make her departure as easy on her sister as possible, and Lily needed Henry more than Sam did in this moment.

Henry stared down at his wife, clearly torn between love and duty. When he straightened, Sam drew in a breath to argue, but his words took the wind from her.

"You're right. I cannot leave her now. There's nothing for it. The carriage is already borrowed, and the tide waits for no one. Kate will have to go."

The lady's maid, who'd come in to check on her mistress, cried out at the same time as Sam, but with greater vehemence.

"I will not be locked up in a contraption with the likes of her, especially not a mechanical one," Kate pronounced. "It's bad enough you ask me to live on an estate where an unrestrained Natural roams. The girl is dangerous, no matter how much you're sweet on her."

Lily dissolved into another bout of coughing so loud and pronounced it brought all conversation to a halt.

The maid ran to Lily's side, bringing with her the bowl of water and damp cloths she'd carried in. "Now see what you've done," she said, glaring at Sam. "What the likes of her did to deserve the likes of you is beyond me."

"Enough." Though he didn't raise his voice, the command in Henry's tone froze both of them. "She is my sister as much as Lily's now, and I will not have you speak to Samantha in this way. You can go pack your bags and move back into your father's cottage. Mister Simmons will find something appropriate for you to do in the fields."

"What?"

Again both Sam and Kate spoke as one, but Sam kept talking.

"Henry, you can't. Lily needs her, and I'm going." Sam crossed to the door. "It won't be a problem any longer. She's only spiteful to me."

If anything, his scowl deepened. "How long has this been going on? I knew you didn't fare well together, but this is more."

Sam shrugged. She hadn't kept the extent of it from him on purpose, but Lily leaned on her maid especially in recent years. "It isn't that bad."

"Bad enough you don't want to share a carriage with her."

Sam waved off the argument. "The coachman knows where to go, doesn't he? It's not like she'll be much use anyway."

Kate harrumphed at that, but Henry shook his head. "You can't go wandering across the country unaccompanied, Samantha. It's not proper."

Despite the stress of Lily's collapse, and the carriage waiting for her outside, Sam burst into laughter, perhaps a bit stronger than necessary.

"Proper should not matter in this," she managed when she could catch a breath. "Where I'm to go, I'll be unaccompanied always." The words sobered her, but still Sam continued, "Really, there's no point in arguing. I refuse to spend that much time trapped with her, and you can't force both of us. You'll just look silly chasing two young women around a carriage. The moment you go after the other, the first of us will just get out."

Henry looked like he would protest then the strength went out of him on a sigh. "If you're sure you'll be all right on your own, there's no time for anything else and nothing more to say."

She could see the gratitude in his eyes as he left to speak with the coachman, but Lily wore a stricken expression, even more pronounced against her pallor.

Sam rushed to her sister's side, ignoring Kate's presence. "It'll be better this way, I promise. You'll rest up, and when you're feeling more like yourself, Henry can take you on a grand tour of the Continent. Who's to question if you make a stop wherever this haven is to be found to rest your horses. Promise me you will."

Lily gave a slow nod, her lips curving in a vain attempt at a smile.

Sam smiled broad enough for the both of them, pulling her sister into a gentle hug. The contact only made her more aware of how frail Lily had grown, but she swallowed hard and made sure none of her thoughts showed when she stepped away.

Henry came through the doorway, Sam's cloak over one arm. "I explained to the driver, and he encourages you to hurry. The carriage is fast, but it takes a bit to get up to full speed. If you run into trouble on the way, having a little extra time might be for the best."

Sam ran to him and hugged her brother-in-law as tight as she could. "You take care of my sister," she commanded against his starched shirt. "Make her well."

Henry tugged Sam away only so he could meet her eye to eye. "Everything in my power I will do for Lily. She holds my heart as well as your own. I swear I'll help her through this, and then we'll take that trip you asked of her."

Startled, she glanced over at her sister, who had lapsed into slumber. When she looked back, Henry smiled. "I overheard you as I came in. It sounds like the perfect thing to do, but we'll wait a bit, for Lily to heal and you to settle in. Now let me hand you up into the carriage and you'd best be off."

It took little time for him to wrap the cloak around her and give her a letter of introduction to his man of business.

Before Sam realized it, she'd descended the steps and climbed into the carriage next to the burbling engine.

Henry leaned in the door and thrust a small leather wallet into her hand. "It's not much, pocket change really, but it's enough to get yourself something to eat if there's time. My man of business will meet you at the port. You have only to show him my letter. He has your papers along with drafts from my bank. Everything you need to make the journey comfortable. I know this wasn't how you expected to start out, or what your sister and I wanted for you, but you're a smart girl. Just listen to what my man tells you, and you'll be on the ship and on your way without trouble. Take care of yourself, Samantha."

He didn't wait for a reply, a lucky choice as Sam didn't think she could have forced words past the tightness in her throat. Instead, she tucked the wallet into her cloak pocket next to the letter and settled onto the cushioned seat.

"Hold on tight, Miss Samantha," the coachman called down from his perch. "It can be a little rough going on until she catches her stride."

Sam gripped the leather strap hanging next to the door with one hand and pulled the curtain back with the other. "I'm set."

She hardly had time to prepare before the carriage lurched into motion, nothing like the horse-drawn conveyances she'd been in before. With the rumble of iron-rimmed wheels against cobblestone then gravel, she raced toward her future, leaving Lily, Henry, and the estate that had become her home behind her faster than Sam would have thought possible.

9

$\mathcal{M}$ orning came with the welcome sight of the port in front of them. Sailors gathered against the rail, those not already sent to take in the sailcloth so they could steam their way in as though they'd used it the whole way. Appearances, as Mister Trupt would have said, were everything.

Nat watched the puffs of man-made clouds drifting from their smokestack instead of the port, his back resting against the wooden bar.

The captain hadn't been wrong about his fascination with the engine, but so far the engineer had shown no sign of softening toward him in particular, though Mister Garth was adamant about needing no help from anyone. If for that aspect alone, Nat sometimes wondered if he should have tried for a position on the tracks, but those were hard to come by and less likely to bring in a real income. Besides, the rails went to the same place every time. A ship could go anywhere.

"There you are, Mister Bowden. You missed breakfast." Captain Paderwatch strolled across the deck, as much at ease as he'd ever seemed on land. His sea legs brought no shame down on his head for all that other aspects of his captaincy might.

Nat raised the pie Jenson had made from the remaining potatoes, scraps of meat, and the last of the flour. "Just doing my part to clear the hold."

"Indeed." The captain barked a laugh. "You are well suited at that. No matter how much goes down your gullet, not a bit sticks to those bones of yours. Maybe it's best your mother doesn't come after all. She'll think I'm feeding you only water and hard tack."

Glancing around to make sure none of the others overheard the captain's comment, Nat stuffed the pie in front of his face in a failed attempt to hide a flush. "No, sir. She'd never think such a thing of you. Mother's nothing but grateful you took me on."

Nat failed to duck the hand Captain Paderwatch put out to muss his hair, a habit developed when he'd been much younger and one he kept hoping the professor would put behind them.

"She's a worrier, your mother, but she raised a fine son."

This time Nat's embarrassment came from a different source, but he turned to stare at the approaching dock anyway, still not wanting the crew to see him color up like a naive lad, as they'd called him two years before when he joined them. "We're almost to the port, Captain. Only two days behind schedule."

A grunt came from beside him as the captain folded his arms on the rail as well. "We wouldn't be that if our engine had a lick of the strength in other ships. It sits poorly with me how we're always tagging in at the end of the line."

Nat twisted to look at the captain then, provoking another laugh.

"You think I'm above such things just because I spend my time with books? Let me share a bit of wisdom I've learned in my journeys. It doesn't matter how far you travel, or what language is spoken at the other end. No one likes to come in last every time. It cuts the heart out of a man, and that's something you never want, not for yourself or for those in your command."

Nat could see the truth in those words, and he'd heard the evidence himself from the lips of the crew even if he hadn't traveled as far afield as the professor in his youth. "But what can we do about it, sir? It's not like the Company has any plans to upgrade this old boat. It's clear enough they'll keep her stumbling around until she can't go any further then let her sink under the waves."

Captain Paderwatch sighed. "You have a good eye for detail, and the ability to put the pieces together all too well. There's nothing we can expect from the Company, but even though late, we've got a bit of a balance from my side of the hold. I've been thinking on this a while now."

Nat nodded as though he could follow the captain's thought, but besides knowing they had no hope, there wasn't much to go on.

"I want you to go into port with Mister Garth today. See if you can't use some of that eye to get us a better deal on the parts Kyle needs to shore up our flagging engine."

"I don't need no help, especially not from the likes of him. Book-learned. Still wet behind the ears he is."

Nat hadn't noticed the engineer's approach despite the hard-soled boots the man wore when most others went barefoot. He jerked, startled by the outburst, but it gave him enough time to swallow his own protest and left him looking the better man of the two.

"Now Kyle, don't be so quick to dismiss the value of a little book learning. I'm sure you'll find Mister Bowden of great help today. I want my coin to stretch as far as it can and our engine to function as best as possible. This young sailor has proved himself useful in many things, not the least of them how he convinced every man here to teach him what he needs to know."

"Every man but this one," Garth muttered into his beard, just loud enough for Nat to hear, but not the captain, who had already strolled away to organize the cargo offload, his posture revealing him to be confident that not only were his decisions final, but the engineer would soon realize the value in Nat's company.

Nat doubted the last, faced as he was with the engineer's glowers. Even if he made a difference, Garth would swallow his own tongue before admitting as much.

"Captain might be taken in by your letters, but don't you expect any favors from me. That engine, no matter how cranky, she's mine to deal with and mine alone. While you were sitting in some book room with a cup of tea, I spent my childhood apprenticed to a boat much like this one, well before steam drove more than the teakettle the crew thinks I don't know they call my engine. Why, I've been on a rocking deck since I could plant both feet beneath me, and no cursed 'educated' man's going to teach me nothing, you hear, *boy*?"

Forcing down the craving to correct his "book room" for "library," Nat kept his mouth firmly shut. Despite his worries, a trip down to the shipyard offered the chance to see not one but many steam engines, most newer and better made than the mysterious contraption that lived in the belly of this ship.

10

he tumult of the morning, both embarking on the journey and seeing for herself just how sick Lily had become, overwhelmed the hum from the carriage engine. She couldn't hear how it spoke of dreams and hopes formed from aether. In the beginning, Sam was able to do nothing more than hold onto the strap with both hands as the steam carriage lurched and rumbled its way to a steady gait, but after a while, she found her head nodding in beat with the wheels.

Round and round the wheels went. Every flaw in the blacksmithing translated into a different note against a road that varied from cobblestone to gravel to dirt and back again as they passed through inn yards and small townships on their way. Sam fought the need for sleep as long as she could then slipped into a doze, half-believing herself awake.

Her head slammed against the carriage wall as they jerked to a halt to the sound of cursing and many raised voices.

She shook herself awake, blinked the sleep from her eyes, and leaned out the window, straining to see what had happened. "Did something break? Is someone hurt?"

The coachman appeared beside her, having jumped down from his seat. "Nothing's broken, miss, at least none that I can tell. It's the curse of rural roads, begging your pardon. Sheep."

No sooner had he identified the problem than Sam's dazed brain correctly translated the sounds she heard from voices into a chorus of high-pitched *'baa's*, an effort assisted by the sight of more than one curly white-and-gray coat bustling around the coachman's trousers.

Sam leaned further to see the road filled with the creatures, milling about in a chaos that lacked only a wolf to become true pandemonium.

From the other side of the coach came a different sound, one distinctly human.

She raced across, the springs bouncing with every step, to discover a young man seated not far from her window, his hand rubbing a visible lump on the side of his head.

"Oh dear me," said the coachman, having completed his circuit to discover the same thing she had. "Are you all right, my good fellow?"

The young man pushed to his feet with the aid of a shepherd's staff and stood there for a moment without speaking, as though getting his bearings.

Just when she thought him steady, a sheep came along behind and butted him with enough force to throw him forward.

Sam stretched both arms out the window to catch him, but the coachman got in the way first.

"Steady on there. Can't have you any more battered than you already are. I swear I never caught sight of you before now." What the coachman's words lacked in sincerity, his tone made up for, the apology clear if only the young shepherd had been listening.

"Oh no. Just look at this mess. Pa will tan my hide if I don't get the flock back together and up to the field before the sun crests the sky. He swore I'd be mucking out pig stalls for the rest of my sorry life if this happened again."

At first his words made little sense, but he'd turned to stare at the mob of sheep, making a bruise on the side of his face visible even as the red died down to form the clear imprint of a hoof.

Sam tsked under her breath, realizing exactly what the shepherd meant by his mutterings. He'd been asleep in the reeds when they'd come storming by. No wonder the sheep had panicked with no hand to guide them or keep them off the road.

"It would serve you right if your Pa did just that," she declared, shocking both men. "Sleeping on the job. Why any number of accidents could have befallen your charges."

He flushed bright red until the bruise vanished under the onslaught and his freckles stood out prominently, revealing him much younger than she'd first thought and younger even than she was.

She shook her head, enjoying the sense of being older when she'd always been the one in trouble before, but she could see nothing would suffice except to help the boy regain his flock.

"We can't be on our way until you get your sheep off the road." Sam stripped her cloak, unhooked the door, and swung down without waiting for the coachman to complete his hasty effort to lower the step. Her freshly polished boots lost some of their shine as a spatter of mud doused them, churned up by the sheep after the morning saw a small rain shower.

She brushed at the edge of her skirt, only succeeding in smearing the mud further. "Well, what are you two gawking at," she said, giving up the effort to gather the cloth in her fists. "Let's get the flock moved over."

Though Sam had watched the farmhands on Henry's estate, she'd never had much to do with sheep directly. They proved the most rascally of beasts.

She spread her skirt and charged them in an effort to drive them off the road, but they scattered every which way, as many startled from the sides back onto the road as she chased off.

After her third try, Sam glanced over to see how the other two were doing, only to find them doubled with laughter.

Sam dropped the edges of her skirt and planted both fists firmly on her hips. Channeling her best imitation of Lily, she scolded them with, "It's all very well to be laughing, but I don't see you succeeding any better at this. And isn't it your hide at risk?" She directed the last at the shepherd, a reminder that produced amazing effects as he gathered himself to the task of collecting his charges.

The coachman joined them, a contrite look cast in her direction and heightened color along his cheekbones.

With the three of them working together, they managed to move every last member of the flock off the road and a safe distance away.

The shepherd thanked them both graciously and promised to keep the sheep away as they started back on their journey.

Sam let the coachman both lower the step and boost her in, unaware until that moment how much the exertion had taken out of her.

"Catch hold," the coachman said only a short time later, and then the carriage started forward once again with the awkward lurching that had signified their first departure.

RYING TO COUNTER THE JERK and roll of the carriage as it gathered speed kept Sam distracted for a good long while. However, once they gained the velocity where their conveyance smoothed its gait, she heard muttered curses again.

The lack of imminent danger made Sam aware of her untidy state, the mud having risen well past the hemline, her hair fallen from its plait, and a distinct musk rising from her skin. She doubted, though, that the coachman cared much about the impression she might make upon their arrival, so his cursing couldn't be for that.

She tapped on the roof of the carriage to catch his attention then leaned out the window to call up, "Is there another problem?"

"It's not one you can solve with a few flaps of your skirt, miss. I'm doing my best."

She began a protest, both of his dismissal and the dodging of her question, when the realization hit her. Sam sank back onto the seat, staring at the dirt under her nails and wool-reddened skin for inspiration.

None came.

They'd been on a tight schedule when they'd started.

With the time wasted getting the sheep off the road, not to mention a second period of building up speed from a dead standstill, they chanced her missing the ship Henry had arranged to take her to the Continent.

Sam stared and stared, but no answer came to her.

If she missed the ship, what then? She couldn't very well go back to Henry's estate, not now. It had taken all her strength to leave the first time, especially with Lily doing so poorly. She wouldn't last another farewell.

Daunted by the task in front of her, Sam pulled out the coin purse Henry had given her and hefted its weight. He'd said it would buy a meal. She had no idea how much a room would cost, or even how to go about getting one.

Her other gift, the letter to Henry's man, came out next.

Sam laid them on the bench beside her, contemplating all she had left to hang her hopes on.

If Henry's man continued to wait even when the ship had sailed, he might be able to help her navigate the streets of

Dover, which might be smaller than London, but Sam had never been on her own. He might help her find a room and might even be able to arrange a different ship.

The list held more might's than surety, and the biggest doubt of all lingered. How could she keep her true nature hidden long enough for those events to occur when she'd be surrounded by the latest in all things mechanical, most crying out as much as the engine still did?

As though to mock her, the landscape beyond the curtain changed into what could only signal the farming outskirts of the port town. So close, but the coachman would have told her if they had made up the lost time. Instead, he'd fallen into glum silence, his efforts to show off the amazing powers of the steam carriage crushed by a dozen or more sheep.

Her thoughts had run full circle, leaving her with nowhere to go. She tucked the purse into her skirt pocket as much to have something to do as a need to secure it. A shiver brought on less by the cold than by her prospects took over, but she lacked the energy to pull on the cloak.

Into that blank moment came a desire, a craving from outside of herself that she'd been doing her best to ignore.

The aether-enhanced engine cried out that it could do so much better, could go so much faster, if she'd only shape the aether and the underlying structure along with it.

Hours before, with the prospect of a hot meal as she embarked on a new, brighter future, Sam had been able to resist the appeals from the engine. She'd held herself back in favor of the chance never to hold back again. But with the coachman's defeat, all those hopes and chances had vanished.

The bout settled over her, a tingling in her fingertips that spread higher and wider until it covered her torso and scalp, and her ears rang with the siren song of transformation waiting to occur.

She did not consciously let it happen, but at the same time she didn't resist very hard either. The risk should have been too great, especially now that they'd reached a more populated area, but the engine's aether-driven promises offered the hope nothing else could.

Her hand pressed against the panel, its latches posing no barrier when faced with her determination. The covering sprang open for her just as it had the proud coachman, releasing a gust of wasted steam. The bright, flashing metal gears spun around as their teeth bit and pushed the carriage wheels down the road.

She could see the answers laid out before her with the glimmer of aether.

Little changes, just tiny adjustments, straightening here, redirecting there. Tangling with the gears while they were turning took all her concentration. Her fingers grew slick with castoff grease, and some of her blood almost joined the lubricant when the teeth came too close and tried to slice into her palm.

Sam did not pull away. She did not stop. She could not.

The transformation held her captive, trapped as securely as she'd locked up the mechanisms she'd created.

A shiver of delight ran down her spine when she realized this mechanism would not be trapped. This one would roam free, seeking her, protecting her if she failed to make the ship. No one would be able to catch her, to seal her away in an asylum where they stashed Naturals for the protection of the wealthy and their toys. No, with this carriage, she'd run ahead of all of them, laughing at their efforts.

The blood pounded through her veins. Her sight grew distinct until she could detect the slightest anomaly, the slightest place where the gears had been thrown off balance or sealed in at an angle no normal craftsman could detect.

One flaw after another, she corrected, she changed, she enhanced, she transformed. This carriage wanted to fly with the winds, and the aether now running between her and the contraption agreed to make it happen. She had only to complete the final adjustment and it would be done.

"There."

Exhausted, Sam slumped back onto the seat, her ears serenaded with the flawless hum of a perfectly tuned engine gathering speed.

11

The trip to the shipyard offered little of the enjoyment Nat had hoped to find on the docks. He followed Mister Garth's path because the stiff-legged engineer would not let him walk abreast, staying close because he did not know the way.

All that changed, though, when they passed through the gate that separated those who rode the decks from those who built them.

Instead of grumbling at having to keep to a subservient place as he had been, now Nat struggled to keep up as distractions abounded. He lingered to watch a hull being built, its bare ribs standing up like the remains of a beached whale. A master carpenter turning planks into the built-in furniture Nat had become so familiar with caught his gaze next. The many other arts being performed all around him proved equally fascinating.

"Wet behind the ears," grumbled Garth.

Nat felt the heat of a flush rise at the truth of the engineer's statement. Still, he'd grown used to Mister Garth's grumbles, and who knew when he'd get the chance to come within the gates again.

"I've got work to do here, boy, and the captain said not to let you out of my sight."

Nat hadn't realized how far the engineer had gone until Garth shouted across the yard to where Nat watched a man using a simple spring-turning machine to wind ropes much faster than even the sailors on his ship could manage.

Though he'd promised himself not to let Garth undermine his enjoyment, he had a hard time letting that comment pass.

"True enough. The captain thought my eye would make sure you returned with the right pieces," he called back, smarting from the public humiliation.

Nat knew he should have clamped his lips shut instead, but the words had already burst out and crossed the open space between them. Where Garth's shout had drawn little attention, carry boys common enough in the yard, Nat's response spoke of the engineer's standing in the eyes of the captain, something every man and boy within hearing would find compelling.

Garth stormed across the space and grabbed Nat by the ear, dragging him toward the back section where metal gleamed before Nat's tear-filled eyes. He knew enough to keep silent this time, though. He'd crossed a line and would take his punishment without protest.

If not, he wouldn't put it past Garth to beat him to a pulp right then and there from the look in the man's face and the way a blood vessel on his high forehead pounded. Without any hair to cover his scalp beyond short tufts, the engineer's state was visible to any who bothered to look. And so many did after Nat's outburst that the least reaction would seem to set the engineer into a rage.

Whether tired of dragging Nat, angry that his efforts produced no result, or aware his behavior drew as much attention as Nat's ill-thought-out call, Garth dropped his hold just before they crossed into the engine area.

Nat swallowed a gasp of relief and straightened to his full height, an inch or more above the engineer's short, broad body. His carefully indrawn breath brought with it scents and even tastes much different from the fresh sawdust and tar sealants of the front shipyard.

Here, the tang of metal filled the air, along with grease so thick his skin felt slimed with it.

Judging rightly that Garth would not appreciate his close proximity, Nat slowed down to peer at a half-assembled engine. He guessed what would have to happen next from engineering diagrams he'd found in the captain's papers, but even so he couldn't visualize the piece or pieces capable of turning this collection of pneumatic gears into something powerful enough to drive a ship across storm-tossed waters.

"Sure is something to look at, isn't it, boy?" The craftsman must have approached while Nat was absorbed in the engine.

"Absolutely. Amazing what this will be capable of once it's all in one piece."

The man gave him an appraising look. "That the way of it then? You one of them autocratic boys turned out to do real work?"

Nat stepped back, aware his tones had given him away. "Something like that," he muttered.

With a nod toward the other section, the craftsman said, "I heard what happened out there, though I don't suppose any of us could very well miss it. Arrogance don't sit well with us."

One toe twisting in the straw-coated dirt on the floor, Nat kept his gaze down. "I didn't mean to be arrogant."

The craftsman took hold of Nat's shoulder with a surprisingly firm grip. "That there's a fine line, 'specially in your type." He shook his head, "But here now, don't be so cowed by a mistake. The measure of a man is not in his book learning or lack of it. You show your worth by what you do, and how you appreciate what I do." The man's solemn expression split into a gap-toothed grin. "You did aright by me. Keep that dumb look going, and you'll have the lot of us eating out of your hand. Not a one doesn't appreciate a visit by some young pluck who can recognize quality when he sees it."

12

As the carriage built up even more speed than before, a whoop of delight came from the coachman.

Sam managed a smile, worn out and starving after her work. She half-lay on the seat, confident her new mechanical would take them to the port with enough time to fill her aching belly.

The speed kept building, faster and faster.

Outside the window, scenery changed from well-spaced farms to more frequent houses, the wheels ringing against hard-packed roads. Then the view grew blurry, and the coachman's cries changed from joy to worried shouts of "Make way."

Sam levered herself upright, the momentum threatening to keep her down.

Houses and businesses flashed by now, showing them entering Dover proper. People jumped from their path with screams, but the carriage barely slowed.

Sam started to worry.

Had she, in her desire to arrive in time, created something too much for the coachman to handle? They showed little sign of easing off their speed, though she caught a wisp of sea salt in the air. The engine only wanted to go fast. It did not care beyond that.

A crack sounded sharp enough to cut through everything else.

The world seemed to freeze for a heartbeat.

Their carriage buckled to one side and rolled half onto the roof before it crashed back down and slid forward despite none of the wheels touching ground.

Sam stared up to see bright blue sky and realized she'd been thrown against the other wall.

She turned her head to find cobblestones but a hands width from her cheek, the edge of the window jouncing and cracking whenever one stone rose higher than the rest. The whole carriage shuddered and groaned, but still did not halt.

Then, with a sickening crunch, they met an immovable object.

Shouting, cursing, screams, and a million other sounds assaulted Sam's ears.

She curled into a ball at the bottom of the carriage and shook with fear.

They would be sure to come for her now. Lily had been right to send her away. She was dangerous. Just look at what she'd done the first time she'd been let out on her own.

"I swear I don't know what happened, officer. I've been driving the steam carriage for weeks now without a problem then all of a sudden it wouldn't stop. It wouldn't slow. It wouldn't do anything but charge ahead. I'm only happy it ran into the side of a building. It could have killed someone."

"Yes, yes, it could have. You'll have to come down to the station with us and give a full report. There will be damages."

"Damages? I'm a simple coachman, officer…"

The voices moved away, taking the coachman with them so she didn't hear the rest, but from the sound of it, the man had forgotten all about her. Sam huddled against the floor, waiting for the police officers to open the carriage and discover what caused this disaster. Though she'd met Henry when he served on the London force, she had little doubt of their reaction to a Natural on the loose. Henry had been special.

After what seemed like forever, Sam opened her eyes to see the same patch of blue above her, or rather a different one with the sun higher in the sky.

No one had searched the carriage. No one came to drag her off to an asylum where she would slowly go mad. No one seemed to be paying the least attention to the carriage or its potential occupants.

She waited a little longer, listening hard to be sure, then climbed the seat as though it were a poorly made ladder. When she reached the top, Sam pushed the door open and poked her head out.

"Hey, you. Get out of there. You've got no business playing in that."

Sam glanced up to see a police uniform and the scowl on top of it.

She shrank back.

"Oh no, you don't. This isn't a play yard for you street children." He lifted her out of the overturned carriage with little difficulty and planted her firmly on the ground. "I don't know how you got past us, but you'd better be on your way right quick or we'll have to take you down to the station."

Though his words made a stern warning, kindness showed in his eyes, enough to tell her she got off lightly.

Sam didn't wait for him to change his mind. "Thank you, Officer," she said in her politest voice then turned and ran through the crowd, the imprint of his startled expression on her memory.

Once she'd achieved some distance, she slowed and finally stopped in an alley to assess her condition.

She'd left her cloak in the carriage and had no idea what had become of the letter, not that she knew how to find Henry's man on her own anyway.

She still had the wallet Henry had given her stuffed in her skirt pocket, but even he'd said it didn't contain much.

Her dirty hands and torn skirt, not to mention the distinct stench of wet sheep, had probably saved her life. The police officer thought her a street child rather than the passenger, or worse the cause. Now, for all practical purposes, she had become a child of the streets.

Her stomach rumbled, breakfast a long way behind her with a lot of hard work between then and now.

Sam realized she had more in common with the street children than just her lack of cleanliness. If she didn't take care, the workhouses would catch her. She'd heard enough of those places from Henry to know they were to be avoided, but she didn't know of any nice person in Dover who would give the burnt or stale breads to the orphan children without anyone to care for them as Lily had in London.

Sam straightened her shoulders and gave herself a mental push to put away tears. She had more than most street children would dream of, especially if she could find Henry's man and her ship.

A salty taste in the air told her she'd stayed down near the docks despite her frantic run. There couldn't be that many ships heading for the Continent. She would just have to search hers out before the tide turned. Surely they'd arrived in time, despite how the carriage ride had ended, and Henry's man would still be waiting for her.

13

Taking the craftsman's advice to heart, Nat allowed himself to be guided from one section of the engine yard to another, always taking care to praise the work before him. He didn't have to try hard as everything they displayed seemed wondrous, from the stamping machine that put out gears with sharp teeth able to join to others of their kind, to the journeymen responsible for filing down those self-same teeth to prevent wear or breakage, and every other step on the path to building a steam engine.

His cheeks felt sore from grinning, and his eyes ached from the many times they'd opened wide in amazement, but Nat wouldn't have traded the experience for a position on the grandest of Her Majesty's fleet.

"And this here is what you need, boy," his guide announced, stopping beside a collection of tools and parts.

Without him realizing it, the steam engineers had been probing him for information on their engine difficulties. Each had offered something of their efforts to enact the repairs and improvements.

Again, Nat felt his lips spread into a grin even as he shook his head in bewilderment. "I've never even seen the engine. How can my words have any meaning? You need to talk to Mister Garth. He's our engineer."

The first craftsman snorted. "He's not worth the least of these parts we're offering you. All telling us what to do and how we're doing it wrong. You've the right of it. Let a man do what he's good for and step out of the way. I tell you these are what you need, and we'll give you a good price as well. Most who come here are like that one, and we can't stomach them. All full of their own importance and belittling ours just because they ride the waters. These are meant for the fancy fleets, but will serve your vessel well enough. Just hope he has more skill with the engine than he does with other engineers."

At that moment, Mister Garth rejoined them, his bald head tinged pink from where his beard ended well up to the curve of his domed skull. "This shipyard's the worst of any I've been to. Not a one can hear what a man has to say. Our captain's going to be disappointed, and he'll hear exactly why." The engineer raised his voice at the last, clearly trying to embarrass the others.

The craftsman who had guided Nat laughed in Mister Garth's face. "Your captain's going to be cheered with the good work this here boy did." He slapped Nat on the back. "Now let us tally up the costs and get you on your way. You make sure to tell him what we said, now, boy. Peter. Yes, you, you lazy carry boy. You help this one out with his load. It's more than one man can carry."

"I'll carry my share," Mister Garth interrupted in an effort to regain some of his standing.

"That you will." The craftsman bundled up the last of the pieces and split the load between Garth and Peter. "This one will lead you back to the ship, as is his right. We'll send the manifest on to your berth."

Garth spluttered and growled his way across the shipyard, Nat keeping out of his sight as a precaution. The men had been good to him, both in letting them have better goods than Garth would have warranted, and in saving face after the disaster of their arrival. Still, the ship didn't have enough space to keep from encountering the engineer.

Besides, Nat still nursed the hope that someday he'd see her engine room, something impossible unless Garth forgot about this humiliation. The sooner the better.

As they passed through the gate, Nat strode forward to split the load properly, but when he tried to take something from Mister Garth, the engineer jerked away.

"Oh, no, you've done enough already, Mister Bowden." He managed to make Nat's name into a curse. "I will not have your hands on my materials. And you'd better keep your nose out of my engine room as well. If I catch you down there even once, I'll grind those pretty fingers between the gears."

14

S am followed her nose to the ships, the salt in the air growing along with the noise as the morning grew near midday and many gathered to take passage. The alleys she followed widened until she could see some distance along them. The packed dirt turned into cobblestones beneath her feet, and storefronts opened onto the streets from which workers eyed her carefully until she'd gone past.

As much as she wanted to say she had money to pay for some of the mouth-watering meat pies displayed before one such store, she knew the quality of Henry's purse would name her a thief even though she came by it honestly. Who would believe her in a tattered dress and grubby hands? Without the coachman or Henry's man of business to vouch for her, even something as simple as a stale roll was out of her reach.

Turning her back on the food she craved took as much strength as ignoring a transformation. Sam looked toward the most unstructured noise in hopes of a distraction.

Random passengers seemed more likely to create chaos than trained workers, and so she'd find Henry's man in that direction.

The victory of her deduction proved short lived as Sam stepped out onto a crowded section of the docks. People of all ages, shapes, and sizes wandered the well-worn boards, elbowing their way through or carrying sharp-edged luggage.

Sam ducked in time to avoid being scraped by a wood box only to bump into an old woman who waved her cane and

screeched something Sam couldn't make out in the over-
whelming cacophony of sound and movement.

A shrill voice called as if for a pet, over and over, piercing
the deeper noise of largely male tones directing, commanding,
and organizing.

Sam glanced at one well-dressed man after another, wondering just how she was to identify the man in Henry's employ.
She dismissed the ones shepherding others, but that still left
more than a handful, and those were only the few visible in a
constantly shifting pageant of passengers.

"Make way," a loud voice said from above her, not offering
enough time to react before a thick hand shoved her hard
enough so Sam stumbled.

The crowd took little notice of her, and she scrambled out
of the way of sharp boots, got her fingers squashed under
lady slippers, and managed to press her back against a wooden
cart wheel that offered some shelter.

Then the cart moved. The safe wheel turned dangerous as
it almost ran over her already bruised fingers.

Sam sprang to her feet, eliciting a startled cry from the cart
man, and dashed toward the ships. Her best chance lay in
learning where each was headed. At least then she'd know
where to look.

She'd barely made it half way to the first gangplank before
someone stepped too close, and she tripped over the out-
thrust boot.

Firm hands gripped her shoulders and put her back on her
feet, but when she turned to offer thanks, the man's scowl terrified her.

She jerked away and ran for the nearest gangplank in the
hopes of finding shelter, but a sailor caught her this time, heft-
ing her off the ground as if she weighed nothing at all. Her

feet kept moving beneath her, but without the ground to push against, she flailed uselessly.

"Can't go any further without a ticket, missy. And I'm guessing you don't have one."

Sam stopped moving entirely except to jerk her head from side to side. "I'm meeting someone. He has my ticket."

The sailor's face creased into so many wrinkles it took a moment for Sam to recognize the smile. "Sure you are, missy. There's better places to look for a patron than down here. These men have themselves fancy ladies. They don't need some flat-chested dock girl. You head further along that way, and you'll find more luck at the worker docks. Get along with you."

He set her down and gave her a light pat on her backside.

Sam twisted, about to protest, but he wagged one finger at her and pointed once again.

Her shoulders sagged with a sigh, and she stepped back into the crowd, knowing no amount of words would convince him. A dock girl didn't sound much better than a street child, though maybe one such as that wouldn't be taken to the workhouses.

Something changed around her, and the press grew greater until Sam felt as though she could hardly breathe. People and luggage shoved her toward the ships and the open water between them. She tried to duck through, then fought, hands thrashing about, but still the crowd surged forward.

Calls, both from the ships and people separated in the crowd, battered her ears along with the thump of many shoes against creaking wood boards, the curses when a foot met another rather than the dock itself, and more noises than she could identify.

She wanted to curl up with her elbows pressed to her ears until they all just went away, but she'd seen what happened to anyone who dropped below the crowd level and had no wish to be trampled twice in one day, or three times if she counted the sheep. She needed to get out, to get free of the crowd, to breathe something other than sweat and salt.

The need built inside her, climbing through her bones and into her throat as a scream that threatened to burst free.

Sam could hear it already, a long, high screech that sounded like "my train." It battered her ears over and over again though Sam could have sworn she'd kept her lips compressed together.

Another shove, and she met a hard wood carton, the frame cutting into her upper back.

Though painful, it offered refuge long enough for Sam to recognize the cry didn't come from her mouth but from a young boy, at least so she guessed. And as soon as she'd made that realization, she heard the train.

Demanding and strident, the command flowed in a path only she could hear. The boy had lost his train, but Sam knew exactly where she could find it, caught between two suitcases not far from where she stood next to the collection of luggage and cargo sailors were busily loading onto the ship behind them. Just as Henry had laid claim to his grandfather's watch, the young boy had carved a connection to his train, making it so much more than a simple toy.

Sam didn't hesitate, any restraint lost in the battering she'd received.

She dove for the toy before it could be lifted into the net with the suitcase that had snagged its string. Her aether-driven fingers snapped the pull cord in two, and she held the train to her chest. Its demand for transformation pounded against her as hard as the noise of the docks. She was no more able to block it out than she'd been the rest.

The baggage offered temporary shelter as she bent to her task, but Sam no longer had the attention to consider such needs. Aether wrapped around her, filling her blood with its desires and none of her own. Despite her hunger, despite the weakness left over from her earlier transformation, she could not resist its call.

Distantly, she knew the crowd kept moving forward. The amount of cartons, crates, and suitcases around her diminished. The boy's frantic cries grew more strident.

None of that mattered.

Her head filled with the train's longing to be able to find its person. Its wish to turn well-crafted wheels under its own power, drawing on the aether as a full-sized train would depend on steam, wiped out everything else.

A detailed plan for these changes stretched out before her, and Sam set to work. She adjusted and changed the mechanism, using the remaining length of rope and some nails pried from the crates to make the train's dreams a reality.

"My train!"

Sam gave a final twist and backed away as the well-dressed young boy raced over to snatch the toy from her. She brushed the hair off her face and raised both hands to show she had no intention of keeping the train.

"Get over here, young man." The face that had frightened Sam before now loomed over the boy with a scowl just as deep.

She half-stepped forward to protect him, but the boy grinned so wide his cheeks must have ached with it and held the train up to show the man.

"My train."

"See that you keep better hold of it this time. We're not going to miss the packet because you've misplaced a toy."

The boy lowered his train so he could clutch it against his chest, some of his delight fading.

A creak and groan sounded a warning behind Sam just as the crate she'd been sheltered by lifted into the air on its way to the ship.

Two things happened all at once.

The crate split, weakened by the nails she'd appropriated to transform the train, and the train began to spin its own wheels in the boy's hands.

The unexpected shift of weight tilted the cargo netting, which only made the crate boards slip more. Fine china that had been packed in straw spilled through the gap, sending a shower of straw and porcelain down on Sam's head.

Even as she ducked the onslaught, she felt more than saw the man wrench the train away, cursing and shouting for help.

At first, Sam thought he wanted help in peeling the boy off his arm, but the way he cast the train from him made Sam remember her sister's warnings.

She'd done it again. Transformed something she should never have touched.

Sam thrust her grease-stained hands beneath the folds of her skirt, but too many had seen her with the toy. She turned to run, clumsy with her hands bound in the cloth.

A sailor caught her before she could hit the ground, his leer and broken-tooth smile failing to comfort her.

Before he could say a word, Sam twisted free to the sound of "catch that thing" coming from behind her. Images of the asylum Henry once described to make sure she understood the danger loomed before Sam's eyes even as she bounced and scrambled her way through the crowd.

Panic undermined her control, and she swerved away from one machine then another, each offering its own request or demand if it had gathered enough aether to strengthen it.

She bumped into a man who pushed her into the arms of another, then spun up against a polished lady who gave a startled cry and stumbled back.

Sam didn't stop to apologize, or even to see the results of her mad dash across the crowded docks. She ducked anyone who called out, unable to know if they meant to help or harm. Even if they would have helped a panicked young girl, what they would do when they discovered her true nature she had no way of telling.

A pain in her side sent Sam palms first into the pavement.

She crawled under a wagon that had stopped there, unable to go any further. Sam had to catch her breath at least, and maybe, just maybe, the passengers who had seen would be more interested in getting aboard the ship than chasing after her.

Now that she could curl into a ball and cover her ears from the noise, Sam no longer wanted that quiet. She wished she could still be there in the crowd, just one more passenger waiting for word that she could mount the gangplank and head for distant places. There was no way she would board her ship now.

She'd never be able to find Henry's man with others looking for her, and even if she did, chances were her ship had been just as eager to catch the tide as the one where the passengers almost trampled her.

But more than missing the ship, Sam felt the pain of the little boy and his train. The toy would always try to find him until someone broke it into little pieces to stop the aether from giving it purpose. And she suspected the boy would mourn its loss long after he'd outgrown all other playthings.

Sam waited for the sounds to die down, for the ships to sail and the dock to clear. She had no idea what she would do next.

Her best chance had been lost, not once but twice because she could not control what Lily persisted in calling a gift. Sam could dredge up no gratitude for her difference. It had cost her everything: Lily, Henry, the estate, and now even the chance to get to the Continent. Her only hope lay in staying hidden, staying in control. And she'd shown just how capable she was of that simple directive. With how luck had been treating her, she'd be locked up before the sun set on this very day.

15

"I'm truly sorry, Mister Garth, for whatever I did to offend you," Nat said, not for the first time as they detoured onto the passenger side of the docks because a wagon blocked the route they'd been taking. "I was only trying to stay out of your way as you requested."

The engineer, who'd steadily ignored Nat since they left the shipyard, twisted around to snarl, "So now you're making it out to be my fault this happened?"

Nat swallowed his retort that they'd attained higher than usual quality—and at a cheaper price—so Garth should be thanking him. Only the machinist's words about arrogance stayed his tongue despite the risks. "Of course not. I would never presume. Only, did you want me to refuse them?"

"Of course not," Garth mocked before he swung back to continue his march forward, a motion so abrupt, the package at the top of his stack started to slip.

"At least let me help." Nat ran up fast enough to catch the bundle before the precious parts could hit the hard ground.

"Get your grasping hands off of my equipment," Garth snarled, his whole face twisted. More bundles shifted, unsettled by the tension in his arms.

Nat raised both hands and backed away. "I'm sorry. It was falling."

"I'm sorry. I'm sorry. Is that all you have to say for yourself. You're a bumbling fool who's puffed up in the head first from your high standing in the old days, and now because some over-themselves engineers thought you a fun toy to wind me up. Keep your mouth shut and get back to the captain's cabin where you belong. Who knows what use he puts to you there?"

Peter shot Nat a sympathetic glance, familiar with this type of treatment, Nat supposed.

"And don't you be thinking of helping that carry boy either. It's his job to carry, and carry he will." Garth had somehow intercepted their look, and now wrestled a hand free despite the precarious balance of his load so he could strip the offending bundle and plunk it on top of Peter's even greater pile. "He'll carry everything all the way onto the ship and down to my engine room as well. You, boy, will be off to the captain as soon as we return, to tell him of your victorious efforts, no doubt. Just as long as you keep out of my hair, I don't much care where you find to stow yourself."

Nat dropped further back, unwilling to get Peter in as much trouble as he found himself, especially not with the smirk he'd caught sight of on the carry boy's face. Garth had little hair to speak of, but he had some sway on the ship. Nat didn't need the crew poisoned against him. Living down his upbringing had been the hardest part of his transition into a trade. Nat had no intention of making that his defining characteristic, and the time spent with the captain, though gaining crew appreciation, did little to help him.

He tried to focus on all the wonders he'd seen rather than the one denied him, but the engine responsible for their safety in storms and their albeit limping progress across the seas remained a mystery he was dying to solve. Even discussing the inner workings of the latest in shipboard steam engines with the shipyard's lead engineer himself offered nothing much of a distraction.

Sure Mister Garth tended to be grumpy with every member of the crew, but the man had taken an unreasonable dislike to Nat from the day he'd first stepped aboard Captain Paderwatch's vessel. Nat would swear up and down he'd done nothing to incur the engineer's animosity, but that one existed could not be denied. Only the captain remained unaware of the problem, as shown by his decision to pair the two of them on this outing. The crewmen were known to lift up tarps when Mister Garth came into sight, laughingly telling Nat to crawl beneath them so he could avoid any chance of an encounter.

A sharp curse sent him out of his glum self-absorption.

He looked up in time to see not one but several men blundering in their direction, the leader having bumped Mister Garth.

"We have to catch it," one cried.

Nat stared in the direction they were streaming, but could see no one, or rather nothing, that matched the admittedly spare description he'd been given. If they chased something, it had long eluded them in the crowd gathered at this section of the passenger docks.

He looked back just in time to see a heavy-set latecomer slam into Peter, sending the top bundle Garth had passed over to punish Nat crashing to the ground. It landed with the harsh clank of abused metal.

"You stupid, clumsy boy," Garth screamed. "Do you have any idea how much I've paid for those? If there's the least bit of bending, you'll be running back to get a new one, you will, and out of your own pocket."

Nat stepped between the two of them. "He had no fault in this, as you well know. He carried too many, especially in a crowd this tight, even without a riot."

Garth snorted. "You call a couple of fellows running after a pickpocket a riot? You really haven't seen much of life, have you? Well, if you're so determined to be noble, you take on half of what he's carrying, and the one that fell too. It'll be your wages docked for any damage."

Peter's grateful look kept Nat's tongue in his mouth when he wanted to point out Mister Garth's own decision had created this situation. Nat would have been happy to carry a third of the load rather than tagging along behind the two of them as though he couldn't be trusted with a single bundle. At least his family didn't depend on his wages, though it seemed unfair for the engineer to blame either of the boys for something out of their control.

The remainder of the journey to the ship passed without incident, and in a silence Nat hoped meant Mister Garth had forgotten the rest of his command.

Sadly, this seemed not to be true as, once they'd boarded, the engineer came to a halt outside the hatch to the engine room rather than continuing forward.

"You put your burden down here and get on with you."

For a heartbeat, Nat thought Garth meant Peter, but when the carry boy started to bend at the knee, Garth barked, "Not you. You have a job to do, one you've shown a piss poor handle of so far. Get your back straight and follow me."

With that, the engineer jerked open the hatch and stomped his way down the short staircase into the belly of the ship, each step resounding with the force of a blow.

Nat let his breath out on a sigh and bent to lower each bundle carefully. He didn't plan to give Mister Garth the least excuse to take more of his pay than necessary, but he'd already lost the one thing he'd hoped to come out of this. The captain had been far off if he'd thought sending Nat with Mister Garth would result in a connection between the two.

Garth kept his hold on the engine so tight it might have been his purse for all he let others even see to it. The engineer did all cleaning and maintenance, bought the supplies, and nursed the machine through each use. Any attempt to infringe on his domain beyond stocking the coal, no matter how innocent, he met with fire and rage. Only luck would keep Peter free of any further abuse before he could escape back to the shipyard and others of better disposition.

16

Afterwhat seemed like forever, the sounds around Sam eased as ship after ship took on its passengers and steamed out of the port. As grateful as she'd been to find the wagon, the space beneath it had grown tight and hot as the sun beat down on the hard-packed dirt making up the road in this section of Dover.

Her stomach growled, demanding sustenance to replace the energy stripped by aether in its need to transform.

She crawled out, took a careful glance around the road, and rose to her feet to shake some of the dust from her once-nice travel dress. Her feet ached in the unaccustomed pinch of boots. Sam braced against the nearest wall, intending to pull them off.

"Get on with you, now. We don't need any of your type up here. Get down to the cargo docks where you belong."

Sam jerked away from the wall. "I was just—"

The shop woman lifted her skirts and ran at Sam much like how Sam had chased Henry's chickens about, only this time she felt as they must have, her heart racing with the need to escape.

She turned and scrambled away, once again running without a clear direction.

By the time her fear faded enough so she could slow to a walking pace, she'd crossed an invisible, but obvious, line somewhere.

The careful shops of the passenger section with their nice clothes and delicacies gave way to tradesman places selling rough-sewn clothing of thick canvas, interspersed with establishments giving off a rancid scent she didn't quite recognize.

Sam thought again of the wallet hidden in her skirts, but even more than before, she could not pull it free here. The few women lounging in the area had a tense, hard-cut look about them, while the men seemed all too interested in her doings for Sam's comfort.

She kept moving, unwilling to stop and chance an encounter she wouldn't know how to get free of, but if anything, the rough nature of her surroundings grew rather than vanishing behind her. No shops stood in this section beyond those reeking of that sour stench, and the few words bawled out from within made her blush more even than the farmhands' speech.

Her feet hurt, her stomach had closed like a fist of pain as hunger ate at her, and sleep beckoned with the strength of a compulsion.

A sailor swaggered out of the nearest door, steam rising from the meat pie in his hand.

Sam couldn't help staring. Her mouth watered in anticipation of food she could not have.

"You want some, girlie?"

"I can pay," she whispered, forgetting the need to keep Henry's wallet hidden.

"I'm sure you can. Just come on over, and I'll show you how to please me."

His eyes changed in a way she'd never seen before, but instinct warned her the consequences would not be worth the food he held pinched between meaty fingers.

"I'm all right," she told him, backing away.

"Oh, I don't think so," came a second voice from behind her. The same sour odor as rose from the taverns wafted past her strong enough to make Sam choke.

Bending in an attempt to find clean air saved her from the thick arms that swept the space where she'd been a moment before.

The second man stumbled, and Sam ducked sideways, remembering the time she'd ventured into the wrong pasture and met with Henry's bull.

Neither sailor had the weight of that massive animal, but they were more agile.

She'd avoided the second, but the move brought her within reach of the first who hoisted her into the air, uncaring for how his hand, coated in grease from the pie, stained the bodice of her dress.

The smell of gravy made Sam faint, but she didn't give in to even that demand beyond a deep longing to wrench the meat pie from his grasp. Instead, she brought up both feet, still encased in the boots she'd come to hate, and slammed them into the face of the second man, now approaching.

He went down cursing, giving Sam a reason to be grateful for the hard-soled footwear Lily expected her to wear.

"Is that the way of it?" growled the first in her ear, his breath no less pungent.

Before Lily put a stop to it, saying Sam had to learn to be a girl, she and Henry had wrestled and played hunting games. Those memories came to her now, along with some of the more rough moves Henry had taught her in the name of fun.

She slammed her elbow back with as much force as she could manage. While it might not have stopped a healthy man, neither of these seemed quite as steady as they should be.

He stumbled and started to fall, dropping her in the process.

Sam kept the presence of mind to snatch what she could of the meat pie from his other hand before she took off at a run, the sound of her boots overly loud to her ears as they pounded against the ground.

Then the tone of their beat changed from a heavy thud to an echoing bang, the meaning of this change filtering through her conscious mind even as she recognized how splashing water eased over the noisy music and shouts from behind her.

She glanced up to see an unattended gangplank, and without thinking twice, she scampered up its length to the deck of a ship tiny when compared to the towering passenger vessels, but still of a good size.

Some boxes arrayed on the boards offered shelter Sam accepted happily. She slipped into a small space left between two of the biggest crates, where neither sailor nor sun could find her, and set to devouring the food she'd stolen. A pang of conscience bit her, but Lily would have wanted those men punished for how they'd manhandled Sam, and taking even the better part of the first one's meat pie seemed mild in comparison to what the police might have done.

Each bite offered a shiver of pleasure unmatched before because she'd never been quite this famished. Still, she had no time to savor. Between her desperate state and the knowledge that she could be discovered at any moment, Sam gobbled down her meal, sucking the last bit of sauce from her fingers and shirt. Not even the grease stains on the fabric from fixing the boy's train could stop her from getting as much as she could from the meal.

"Get those stowed before you take a night on shore. We're sailing tomorrow with the tide."

Sam flattened against the crate when she heard a voice not far from her.

A crate near those forming her shelter grated against the wood of the deck as the sailors she couldn't see moved it.

"Wait, not those. The captain wants that group near the front. Has a plan for offloading them when we stop for supplies. Start with these over here. Nat, you get down in the hold and make sure the space is clear."

Sam held her breath as she waited to discover if the command meant she had gained or lost time.

When the noises seemed to grow more distant, she peeked around the edge to see the sailors concentrating on a section more toward the middle of the ship. Sam looked up and down the deck for a better hiding place. A closed hatch stood off to one side where she could see no sailors.

She hesitated, debating between running down the plank again and making another attempt to find Henry's man as compared to stowing away on a ship bound who knew where.

Memory of her close escapes on the docks, along with having no idea how to find the man, decided her. At least she'd made it on a ship. Anywhere might be safer for a Natural than England.

Sam crept around the crates, keeping them or one of the smaller rowboats between her and the crew as much as she could. The last stretch, though, lay bare of any cover. She didn't want to think about what they would do with her if they discovered her presence, even without knowing her nature, but she had no options left. She'd moved too far from the plank to reach it before being caught even if she'd wanted to go back into that confusing world where everyone seemed a threat.

A quick gasp of air, and she dove across the open space, grateful the scraping of heavy wooden crates masked the thump of her boots though she wished she'd thought to take them off.

None of the sailors seemed to notice her presence, and she reached the hatch without raising an alarm. Still, now she had to brave whatever lay on the other side.

The handle jerked out of her grasp, giving Sam hardly enough time to dive behind and press herself flat.

"That's the last of it, boy, and you were lucky. Or should I say Mister Bowden was lucky. There's no damage from the spill. You should be more careful with your next task, or you may not get off so lightly."

The lanky, dark-haired boy who followed grimaced behind the stout man's back, as though to say this version of punishment had been hard enough for his tastes.

Sam wondered at her choice to put herself in the man's control, but the decision had been made. She only waited for the two of them to pass far enough from earshot for her to slip within.

Her second step almost sent her pitching forward as what she'd thought to be a floor vanished beneath her feet. She flung her arms wide and found a banner of sorts, though its cold, metal surface sent shivers down her spine even as her curled fingers identified it to be a pipe.

She stood there as though suspended above a chasm. Little light filtered in through the hatch above, and she could see no portholes bringing in the fading sun either.

Her eyes took a long time to adjust, and still offered only a vague sense of the space, enough to tell her she'd found no small cabin. The darkness stretched off in all directions, a looming presence.

But where the darkness might have scared many young girls, Sam had spent much of her childhood hiding in closets or in dark places like the barn Lily had found to shelter her. Sometimes she had a lamp, and sometimes not. The need to conserve fuel, though, often made her hesitate to light one when she did have it.

That history helped her find the courage now to step down into the chamber and feel her way across a room that offered obstacles of many shapes and sizes. Most she could identify as either wooden crates or different types of metal, some sheets and some pipes like those she'd used to guide her down the steps. What she found there made no sense until she realized the awkward collection could only mean she'd stumbled upon one of the cargo holds.

A better place to hide she could not imagine, but still, Sam made sure she squirmed her way between many layers of pipes until she found a small gap braced on one side by a wooden wall. Here she could listen to the slap of waves produced either by wind or the passage of the many steam vessels that had filled the docks. The sound itself offered enough of a soothing melody to set Sam to yawning.

She pulled off the boots to relieve her pinched feet and tucked Henry's wallet away in them as well. She'd need both on the Continent, but not likely before then. Her eyes slipped closed, and she decided to worry about food and the like come morning. At least she'd found passage of a sort.

Dreams filled with squeaks and hisses overwhelmed her, but nothing could break the exhaustion that lay claim to every bit of her consciousness.

17

Every muscle in Nat's body ached from shifting cargo and reorganizing the holds as each new load came in. The captain marked all his purchases with a stripe of ocher as was the tradition for the captain's share, and they had to tuck every last bit of the marked crates and bundles into the area of the hold kept separate. Though this extra effort raised grumbles on other ships from what the rest of the crew said, never on theirs. Captain Paderwatch shared the earnings from his choices with all of them, recognizing none of that benefit would come to him without their help.

Still, Nat released a grateful sigh when the piles of official and captain's cargo had all vanished into the hold and been stowed away for their departure. Morning would come all too quickly as the night had grown long. Much of the last work had been done under lamplight.

"Ah, there you are Mister Bowden."

Nat froze at the sound of the captain's voice, but he knew he could not ignore the summons no matter how much he longed for his hammock. He gritted his teeth and refused to complain as the captain waved him toward the cabin.

"I want to go over my plan for the morning. You make a better sounding board than my books."

Nat managed a weak laugh at the familiar joke, but his future depended on Captain Paderwatch's perceptions about him. He was determined not to give any of the crew, especially their captain, a reason to complain.

"Sit yourself down over there where you can see the charts well."

Without a word, not that he could be sure to manage a coherent sentence, Nat sank onto the bench and propped his chin with both hands, staring down at the charts as though his mind could make any sense of them.

The captain tapped a chart in front of Nat. "This here is the Dover port. I've been checking the tides against the almanac, and they'll be drawing out a good four bells before when we were told. Most of the other ships will spend their morning loading and sorting cargo, but not us. We can get underway on this early tide, though it might not be enough to move one of the bigger ships. Sometimes it's an advantage to be so small. Our size makes us nimble. The equipment might belong to an earlier age, but we can still succeed through better planning. I've put aside some choice items in my part of the hold. If we can make port before any others from this part of the world, we'll fetch a pretty penny for those goods."

Nat's thoughts drifted, wondering just what the captain had settled on this time, and which port would be their first destination on this voyage. His eyes slipped closed, and his chin sank further toward the table.

A sharp clap on his shoulder sent Nat scrambling to his feet.

The captain only laughed. "You make a grand listener even when you're asleep where you stand, or sit in this case. But for this to work, we need a well-rested crew. I count you in that number so shouldn't keep you here when the others have gone to find their rest. Now wipe the drool from your chin and go curl in your blankets. Early morning tomorrow. We'll be up before the sun rises for sure."

Nat blinked wearily at the captain's enthusiasm, his sleeve rubbing against his chin.

"Go on with you. You'll do me no good asleep on the rig-gings."

Stumbling on his way to his hammock, the captain's speech filtered through Nat's sleep-dazed brain and he couldn't help but see the brilliance in it. The crew might see the professor as a nominal leader worth nothing more than keeping the Company officials happy, but all that book learning opened up strategies another captain and crew might not have thought about. Even if they had, they wouldn't know enough about every place the Company sent them so as to choose just what would be in greatest demand.

He fell asleep with a faint smile curling his lips. The ship might be old, and the crew old-fashioned, but he saw more of a future here than on a bigger steamship where he'd be one of many cabin boys and the captain would never think to bring him in to consider plans.

18

No light shone in her room when Sam woke, but she'd often come alert before the sun, especially with the winter just past. She stretched an arm over her head, grasping for the blanket with her other.

Her raised hand smacked into cold metal while she could only find dirty cloth beneath the other.

The events of the previous day came flooding back, and she drew both knees to her chest, shivering as much with the change in her fortunes as the early morning chill. What had seemed so clever an idea in the flush of aether-borne hunger now fell to pieces beneath her.

Despite what she'd thought the previous night, she had to get off the ship.

Sam had no supplies to keep herself hidden, and whatever the charge for being found out stowing away, the penalties would be higher once they figured out what she must be. Starving, she would be unable to control her urges.

Even worse, if they could trace her back to Lily and Henry, her family would pay the price for her failure.

A low groan cut through her frantic thoughts, so close that she first thought another lay hidden in this storage room.

Then the pipe pressed against her side groaned again, and its chilled surface began to heat.

She jerked away and took another look around her now that her eyes had adjusted to use what little light seeped in between the cracks in the ceiling despite the tar she could see staining between them.

The pipes she'd crawled through to get to this corner resembled less the careful storage of cargo and more a haphazard alignment of copper pathways rising from the floor to trace across the ceiling and at every possible height, stretching from one side of the room to the other, with no sign of an end. If she had to guess, Sam would say the pipes did not stop there either, but pierced the very walls to wind their way into every part of the ship, carrying steam to power other machinery or drawing water back to this very room.

Her heart thumped its way through a beat or two before she lost control and turned to face what she'd been too frightened and exhausted to notice the previous day. The distant engine called to her with whistles, groans, and clicks, its worn gearage and poorly aligned tracks begging her to help.

Like the carriage, this machine, the heart of the steamship, did not crave transformation into something different. It loved this purpose, longed for it, but wanted to be so much better at the task the universe had set to its conjunction of moving parts. Aether had gathered here for an age, possibly longer than the fifteen years Sam had walked this earth, hoping, praying even, that someday it would gather enough to reach the ears of one who could hear its cries.

The need dragged at her, pulling both body and soul toward the steam engine. Aether stretched along the pipes that surrounded her, racing toward her and seeping into Sam until her arms tingled with the strength of it, greater than anything she'd felt before.

Her fingers closed on a bundle of gears left strewn across the floor below the steps before she even knew she'd moved out of her hiding place. She undid the knots of fabric and pulled a gear free to press the metal to her palm.

Sam absorbed its shape even as she saw the exact location where it was needed to replace a part with worn teeth. She had never transformed anything as complex as the machine that called her now, but its wealth of aether offered guidance, direction not just for where to place the gear, but how to link it in and balance the mechanism so each tooth fit smoothly with the gears around it.

She rose out of a half-crouch and took a step toward the massive construct on the far side of the room.

Its metal shape soared to the ceiling where the top of the boiler joined with pipes that hung from the rafters and connected everything on the ship to this one room. The heart cried out to her, pushing aside her hesitation in its demand to be whole, but more than that, it wanted to be better. The engine held enough aether to have become half-sentient the way a mechanical man could be. It heard the grumbles of its crew. It knew they needed more.

Aether drove this knowledge into Sam as a series of impressions, flashes carrying with them snippets of conversations spoken over the years this ship had gathered awareness.

It knew every member of the crew: their strengths, weaknesses, flaws, and moments of brilliance. All of this the engine pushed at her, using not just its desires, but those of the crew to shape her will.

Sam had never been so manipulated, not by her family nor a machine, and she wasn't about to start now. She dropped the gear to the floor with a thud and stepped away, heading back toward her hiding spot.

The engine let out a shriek of steam loud enough to make Sam clap her hands to both ears in a belated attempt to dampen the piercing cry. Her mechanicals had never battered her so. They'd always asked kindly when wanting a change.

Tears sprung into her eyes as she longed to be back in her workshop surrounded by her own machines, ones who loved her as much as she did them.

When the noise finally stopped, the silence seemed deafening, at least until she heard the heavy thud of running steps.

Fear cut through her misery, and Sam dove between the nearest pipes just in time as the hatch slammed open and thin sunlight poured in. She pressed her body to the floor, knowing she couldn't chance crawling the rest of the way back to her nest, not with someone coming down the stairs and looking into the chamber.

"What's wrong with it this time?" an unfamiliar voice asked.

"I'll have to check her out, Captain. It'll take some time."

That voice she knew all too well from hearing him tell off the black-haired boy the previous day. She could not afford to be found by such a man. He seemed to have no kindness in his soul.

"Well, make quick about it, Garth. Much rests on us sailing a good number of hours before the others headed in the same direction, especially with the engine acting up. Doesn't help that it probably woke the crew of at least the vessels on either side if not the whole dock."

Perhaps the last had not been meant to be overheard from the lowered tone, but the hatchway amplified the captain's voice so both Sam and the angry man could hear it easily. A flash of sympathy toward the man surprised Sam with what she knew of him, but perhaps he had cause to be grumpy.

"That blasted carry-boy. I let him off too easily. Just look at this mess. Here I thought he'd placed the bundles well, but this one must have fallen with enough force to break open. Or maybe that arrogant shipbuilder didn't bother securing the ties, and I'm lucky we didn't leave pieces strewn across the whole dock for pickpockets to claim."

He continued to mutter a litany of accusations and curses against any and every person who'd come in contact with the gear, the name Nat showing up more than once, but Sam tried to tune him out along with the other demand on her attention.

The engine had learned from its mistakes. Any subtlety had left its efforts, and demand as well. Instead, it laid bare the dreams harbored in each puff of aether and begged her to help. It spoke of a solitude she knew all too well, and of knowing a better future but being unable to reach it.

Sam thought for a moment it read her own life and dreams then realized she could not be alone in having her wishes held captive by forces beyond her control. A kinship grew between them in the time it took the engineer, for that was what he must have been, to gather his tools and the parts he thought would be necessary.

She shifted so she could watch him, the process he used almost painful to see when she knew how it should have been done.

Sam flinched when the engineer pounded a fresh gear into place, feeling the scrape and grind of the gears as though he tortured her, not the engine. She struggled to recognize the man did his best without aether to assist and guided only by sight, but soon she could no longer tolerate the double vision.

When he started pounding another gear, Sam rolled onto her hands and knees, and crept back to her hiding spot. Hunger gnawed a hole in her stomach where the engine had stripped the value from the meat pie she'd stolen. Sam drew her knees to her chest, trying to ignore both the banging and her stomach.

Any chance of sneaking off the ship had ended with the engine's scream and the captain's demand. The engineer would work on the engine until it managed enough to get the ship away from the dock, at which point she'd have no hope of escape, even ignoring the thumps and thuds on the ceiling above her, a clear sign the ship itself was now fully awake. The open space she'd crossed when they were distracted would give her away to the nearest sailor now, if he paid even the slightest attention to his surroundings. And from the sound of it, the sailors were everywhere this morning.

She curled around her aching stomach and wondered just how bad a ship's rat would taste raw. Perhaps if the pipes grew hot enough, she could cook the meat a little bit, though the smell might draw too much attention.

If she could even find the strength to catch one.

19

Nat stumbled into the kitchen, scrubbing the sleep out of both eyes with the back of his hand. It felt as if he'd just rested his head on the folded shirt he used for a pillow when he'd been woken by what sounded as though a thousand seagulls had taken to the sky to fight over a single fish.

The sun already crested the horizon, spreading a splash of red, orange, and yellow across the water, and the captain had wanted an early weigh anchor.

"You just set down there before you topple over into my porridge," Jenson said the moment he caught sight of Nat. "I'll put together a plate for you in a bit. I'm dishing out some for Mister Garth on the captain's order."

Sinking onto the same stool he'd used often enough in helping prepare the meals, Nat fought the desire to rest his head on folded arms, an act that would be sure to send him back into slumber. Then Jenson's odd sentence caught up to him, along with the lack of a sour tone.

"Since when does Mister Garth rate a meal in his cabin?"

Jenson, who'd never been one to miss a sharp comment, just shook his head. "Not his cabin, boy, the engine room. Don't tell me you slept through the death knell of our ship, now did you?"

"The engine room?"

"You becoming some type of a parrot? Can't say as I've seen much use for them aboard ship, and certainly not in my kitchen."

Nat forced his sluggish mind to review what he'd been told. Not seagulls but the engine. Soon, Jenson would be looking for someone to deliver Mister Garth's meal while he got back to the task of getting the rest of the crew fed.

"I'll take it." The words were out of his mouth almost before he'd recognized the chance to see what lay behind that hatch, along with the hope of undoing some of the damage his enthusiasm had caused the day before.

Jenson laughed. "You? You can hardly stand on your own two feet and haven't had anything to line that empty stomach of yours. I heard some of the others talking about how the captain kept you going long past the rest of the crew, and after a full day shifting cargo on top. No, rest a bit. You won't have much hope of easing off your feet once Mister Garth gets that engine turning over."

Nat jumped up with twice the energy he'd shown on his arrival. "I'll eat after, I swear. Let me take it. There's no harm in it, I promise you. I just want to see the engine room. Please?"

Jenson stared at him for so long Nat thought the cook would hold fast or the meal would grow cold, but then he nodded once. "Far be it for me to stand between a boy and his curiosity. You take care now and don't do anything to distract the engineer though. The captain will have both our heads if you get Garth all twisted up about something beyond fixing the teakettle so we can ship out, you hear me?"

"I promise. I swear. I'll be the soul of helpful. I won't say one word wrong, or maybe not a word at all if that'll do best."

With another bark of laughter, Jenson handed over a shallow, curved plate with a healthy portion of porridge and a fresh roll stuck into the gray mass. "Don't be so quick with your promises or your swears, boy. Hasn't Mister Trupt told you that often enough? Just keep a level head and bring the man his food. You don't have to swallow your tongue. Just school it a bit. He's the master of that domain as much as I am of this one."

Nat tucked the plate close so he wouldn't spill any. "Right. Thanks." He didn't even look at the cook as he headed for the doorway, unable to hold back a grin.

The engine room. Finally.

*N*OT WANTING TO WORSEN THE situation, Nat rapped sharply on the hatch to get Mister Garth's attention, but though he leaned against the wood, an awkward position with the porridge in his hands, he heard no response. The noises from below must have masked his effort to be polite.

Nat lifted the hatch, seeing no other choice.

The top step creaked when he moved onto it.

"What are you doing here? Didn't I tell you never to set one foot in my engine room?"

The harsh bark startled him, and he struggled to keep the plate from falling or the generous portion of porridge from sloshing over the edge. "Jenson sent me," he managed after regaining control of his voice. "With breakfast since you're in here working so hard." If the engineer thought he'd been commanded, maybe that would soften his objections.

Movement away from him toward the interior of a room filled with pipes going in every direction caught Nat's attention, but the lamp Garth used offered too little illumination from this angle to reveal much of the space Nat longed to see. The engineer must have come to see who was knocking.

He went down two more steps, accepting the silence as some sort of a backhanded removal of his restriction. Most men could be bought by their stomachs, at least when they gave up something small.

"Just what do you think you're doing? Have all those books done damage to your hearing, boy? You are not to come down here. I don't care if the Queen herself bids you to. Get out."

Nat didn't know how the engineer could see that he'd moved, but it seemed even food would do little to change the man's mind. He strained to see something of the room from where he stood, but without disobeying and charging down the steps, he had little hope. Nat could tell if he went even one step further, any chance of reconciling with Mister Garth would be destroyed forever.

Sighing, he lowered the dish to a crate he could reach through the railing. "All right, then. I'm going. Your breakfast is here by the stair. You might want to eat it before the porridge gets cold."

A wordless growl, accompanied by the ping of hammer against metal came as Nat's only reply. He winced to hear the ping repeat even louder, sure the object receiving Mister Garth's not so gentle attention would fare poorly. At least the hammer didn't land on Nat's fingers, as the engineer most likely imagined.

He'd done nothing on purpose to antagonize the man, but it seemed every act had that result no matter what his intention.

A weak hope that the food would soften the engineer toward him was all Nat could manage as he went back up on deck to seek his own sustenance. His stomach felt shriveled as though it had given up any belief he'd be so good as to put food down his throat. Nat knew full well there'd be little time for him to eat once they got underway. The captain had no intention of missing the early tide, and it would be some time after before the sails were set and the course steady enough to break for lunch.

20

Sam had remained crouched in the far corner as she listened to the argument, if such a one-sided exchange
could be called that. At least the engineer had not caught her
this morning. If he proved so unwilling toward one bringing
him food, how much harsher would he treat a stowaway, inten-
tional or not, especially one with some of his materials in her
hand.

Steam rushing through the pipes around her masked what
noise she made, not that it mattered with the sharp banging
the engineer produced when he wasn't cursing worse than
Henry's farm workers each time they thought she wasn't
around to hear.

She winced at a particularly strong blow, the force vibrating
along the pipe supporting her shoulder.

If he didn't take care, he'd loosen every joint of the old
engine and cause many more problems than he'd come down
here to fix. She didn't fault his dedication, just his methods.

Her mind clung to the last thought until she recognized its
meaning.

The sounds of his labors had not changed since the boy
brought a plate of porridge she could just see from her hiding
spot. Steam still rose from its surface, adding a rich, nutty
scent to the tang of metal mixed with overheated seawater.

She waited a bit longer to see if the man would take his
meal as soon as the boy he'd been so rude to had moved out

of earshot, but nothing in the rhythms of blows or curses showed any sign of lessening.

The steam taunted her, unconfined as it was in the spaces between the pipes. Its scent wafted in her direction, the air chill enough to show curls of white waving their temptation at her, enticing her forward.

Her stomach grumbled loudly in her ears, but the engineer's curse rang louder.

If she waited too long, he'd pause.

If she timed it poorly, he'd catch sight of her where no one should be, and she'd seen his reaction to intruders already.

The only other option, for however long the journey lasted, would be any rats she could catch, raw and unskinned.

She'd been hungry before, but always Lily had brought her something even when the times were rough. This hunger bit all the deeper for the knowledge Lily was not here and never would be again. She'd said she could fend for herself, and now she had to prove it. Sam refused to fail her first test and would much rather pilfer the cooling porridge than gnaw on raw meat from vermin.

A glance toward the engine showed no sign of the engineer, his voice muffled as though he'd gone around the back or crawled into the huge machine to reach another location for his brutal care. She'd have no better chance than this.

Sam dove between the pipes, knowing caution would cost her time she could ill afford.

Her knee struck a pipe hard enough to collapse her joint, but she rolled with the fall, using the momentum to propel her body across the small gap between her and the plate that had become her sole focus.

She could do nothing now to prevent discovery. Only fate, and whatever damage had seized the engine, could save her now. At least if they caught her she'd go to the asylum with a full stomach.

Both hands sank into the coarse porridge, her fingers singed by the heat it still retained. She didn't slow down, though, shoveling as much into her mouth as she could, chewing rapidly, and swallowing in time to add another load to her tongue.

The food had little of the complex spices Cook used to tease the palate, but nothing had ever tasted better as she gulped it down as fast as she could manage.

The meal sat heavy in her stomach, and Sam burped, having swallowed almost as much air as sustenance. She could have kept going and even licked the plate clean, but a good layer and the roll remained in the plate. The effort to back away exhausted her, especially since she had no guarantee of another meal until the ship came to rest in a different port and she could make her escape. But her hiding spot only worked because no one thought to search the back sides of the engine room.

The engineer had not seen the amount when the boy brought his food. He'd been too busy working and giving the boy a firm lashing with his tongue.

As long as she'd left no evidence, he had little cause to suspect a stowaway had swallowed down more than half the generous portion offered him.

She knew the reasoning to be sound, but still, returning to her hiding place without taking at least the roll hurt. Despite the dust collected on her fingers, Sam licked each one clean, then climbed back to do the same to the pipes when she realized she'd left a path. This existence had little in common with the one she'd left. Though her life had been difficult before Henry discovered the truth and took both of them in, she'd had Lily then. Now she had only herself.

Homesickness and a longing for her sister hit Sam with the force of a blow. She smothered a whimper, shoving a fist into her mouth and biting down hard enough to hurt.

She had to be strong, for herself, but also for Lily. Her sister needed time and care to heal. She refused to believe Lily had been telling the truth to Henry, preferring his version of her sister's sickness. If Sam had stayed at the estate, Lily would have done nothing but worry and fuss, taking more care for Sam than she ever did for herself though she had the greater need.

Lily required this, but so did Sam. She needed to take control and become what she was intended to be. She couldn't forever live as an addition to Henry and Lily's life. She needed to make her own way. And though this had not been how she'd intended to start, the fact remained that she'd managed to gain passage away from Dover to some distant land. From there she'd make her way to the places where Naturals could be free. Surely she could manage that much once she touched down on soil where there were fewer restrictions than in England itself.

Keeping that thought at the front of her mind, Sam curled around her distended belly and allowed herself to drift back to sleep. She had nothing else to do, and asleep, she would be less likely to get into trouble she would not be able to get out of.

If she could just stay hidden until the ship had left the port, what could they do with her except kick her off at the next landing? And from the urgency the engineer gave his repairs, she didn't imagine they'd be lingering here much longer.

21

The whistle calling all hands to the ropes came when Nat had barely snatched a few bites of the already congealed porridge Jenson had left for him when feeding the rest of the crew. His stomach grumbled with the memory even as he scrambled up the lines to join Phil in stringing up the sails.

Though a concession to the damage, and a loss of face before all the captains in Dover, Captain Paderwatch had decided to give up on Mister Garth and the chance of a repaired engine. They would sail out of port in the style of older vessels, with cloth aiding the tide.

Even the newest of the steamships used the water's draw when heading out to sea, but their sails stayed furled, if they even had any. The crew liked to hide their dependency as much as possible with minimal sail and visible steam clouds from the pipe.

This time, they left with full sheets and no telltale white rising from their vents.

Nat did his share of grumbling.

Mister Garth could have had the decency to vent some steam while he worked to maintain the illusion. The boiler had been active when he'd brought the ungrateful man his breakfast, so it wasn't as if steam would have been hard to come by. It might have helped the engineer to ease the pressure in his system, not that his blows indicated a focus on delicate adjustment.

But Mister Garth had stomped across the deck to his cabin some time ago without any sign of steam or movement from the paddles.

The need to gloat at Mister Garth's failure vied with Nat's frustration at a further destruction of their reputation. It didn't matter how well the captain used his knowledge to earn the crew a little extra if they only got the worst cargo runs. Who would trust an unreliable sailing ship when all others could steam their way through lulls and even fierce storms.

"Now, now, Mister Bowden. Don't be dwelling on things you can't change. Concentrate instead on what you can. Tie that rope off properly and help me adjust the sail."

Nat glanced up to see Phil shaking his head at the piss-poor job Nat had done, his mind elsewhere.

A flush heated the back of his neck as if he'd gotten too much sun, but Nat didn't argue as he undid his work and started again.

He ignored his grumbling stomach even though hunger made his gut feel plastered against his spine. He'd taken an opportunity in bringing Mister Garth a meal and it cost him. He couldn't regret the choice, though. Enough kindness could turn that sour engineer into a mentor, maybe even a friend. If going hungry could gain him access to the engine room, then he'd go hungry.

Meanwhile, he planned to ensure not a single member of the crew could doubt his enthusiasm and value. He might be the lowest crewmember on what was arguable the lowest vessel in the Company's merchant fleet, but he took pride in his work, and he'd learned a lot since the first day he shipped out to the sight of his mother weeping on the docks.

The rhythm of getting their vessel out to sea and steady on course soon took over and distracted him from both his morning failure and the lack of food lining his stomach. The crew had taught him so much already. He took every opportunity to prove he'd listened and learned. He leapt into each task with enthusiasm and care, determined not a man among them could have a complaint.

THEY'D SWEPT PAST THE LAST ship a long time ago, the tide pulling and wind filling every square inch of cloth to drive their steamship along. Waves smacked the sides, and from his vantage point up in the rigging, Nat could see fish begin to leap the foam of their wake.

This had been why he'd wanted the sea over a train. Not the opportunities—though that's what he'd told his mother—but for the freedom to see the world and to fly across the water with clear skies and full sails.

"That's the way of it, men. Get yourself down and stretch a while. Jenson might even have a bite to sup on," Mister Trupt called, waving them down.

Nat shook off the siren call of the sea and remembered his grumbling stomach in the same moment. He scrambled down the ropes, getting a pat and a laugh from Phil on his way.

"Looks like you've gained your craft, Nat," the rigger called as he went by. "A full on rope rat you've become."

Waiting until his feet landed on the rocking deck, Nat flashed Phil a grin. "If I have, it's your teaching made it happen."

A hand closed on his shoulder, but rather than the compliment he'd been expecting, the touch tightened hard enough to make him wince.

Nat twisted to see his tormentor, stunned to find the good-natured cook instead of Mister Trupt with some complaint.

Jenson scowled down at him. "I told you food would be waiting, and it had been. If it were cold, that was your own choice in going after Mister Garth."

Nat shrugged off the touch. "I meant to finish it. I would have, but the whistle sounded. I wouldn't have left it if I didn't have to." He hadn't expected the cook to question his decision. Surely a veteran of the seas knew a sailor didn't hesitate when called to duty.

"You hardly touched it, but the call had nothing to do with that, and you know it."

Nat's brows lowered as he tried to make out the cook's meaning. "I don't scorn your cooking. You should know that by now. It's hearty and filling."

"And you like yours piping hot."

"Of course. Who wouldn't?"

The other sailors gathered round. Their confrontation proved as interesting as any other diversion in one of the few chances for rest before the first mate found work for all those not asleep.

Jenson thrust both fists onto his hips. "And if I left food for you as I promised while I went to see to the rest of the men, I suppose it would have been too cold for you then?"

Nat couldn't see where the conversation was going, and he'd started losing patience. Who, or what, had turned the cook against him? "It was good enough to line my belly, but that's what time I had."

"You had time enough to swallow down half of Mister's Garth's portion, though, didn't you?"

The statement, delivered with such an adamant tone, struck Nat dumb. He stared at the glowering cook and gave his head a slow shake. "What are you talking about?"

Jenson poked Nat in the chest. "I'm talking about leaving me to take the blame for giving Mister Garth a stingy serving when I filled that plate so high you had trouble carrying it, that's what I mean. No wonder you had no stomach for your portion after gobbling up his, and just because he wouldn't let you see his engine room. Don't you know there's no greater crime than to take a man's food? You think being a boy will save you, and this time it might, but a man's actions show his true nature, not his words. You should remember that if you ever want to be seen as more than a wealthy boy playing at working a true hand."

With that, the cook pivoted and stomped off, each footfall resounding with a heavy thud.

Rage welled up in Nat greater than he'd ever felt. It was not enough for the engineer to take credit for the quality of the goods Nat had won them, but to poison the crew against him was an action without excuse. To accuse him of theft, and of food even. On a different ship than this, that would be a flogging offense. Even here, the crew would never trust someone who would deprive others to act the glutton.

He shoved one of the gawkers out of the way as he marched toward the hatch of the engine room. All thought of currying Mister Garth's favor had been wiped out with this action. Nat didn't care if he never saw the engine in a lifetime of service. He could not let this stand.

"Slow down there, Mister Bowden." Mister Trupt caught Nat by the back of the shirt. "Whatever you're thinking, it'll do you no good, boy. Don't go causing trouble."

Nat jerked against the hold. "Did you hear what he said? What Mister Garth told him?" He spat the name.

Mister Trupt had the audacity to laugh. "Aye. I heard and so did all of the ship. I doubt a one of them believed it though."

"Jenson did." Nat couldn't keep the petulance from his tone.

The first mate shook his head. "Maybe he did right now with Garth's accusations ringing in his ears, but if you give the man some time to cool, he'll realize your actions have shown often enough that you think of others many times before yourself. But if you make a war of this tussle, it'll never fade away."

"He can't say that about me. I don't care what you want. I'll not have the crew thinking I'd let such a slight stand."

Mister Trupt shook Nat hard by the shoulders. "Think, boy. Has all your book learning taught you nothing?"

Nat stilled, caught more by the first mate's tone than his actual words.

"That's better. I knew there was more than wool between your ears." Trupt allowed himself a slight smile. "Who do you think the captain needs more? A cabin boy, or the engineer?"

"Professor Paderwatch would never—"

"The professor might not, considering your family connections and all, but he's more than a professor now. Do you think he would jeopardize all of us just to protect a prideful boy who couldn't recognize when best to back down? You think we could manage another engineer? I don't know what Mister Garth did to anger the Company, but we're lucky to have someone who knows one end of a hammer from another to nurse the teakettle. You think you could do as good a job? Because I sure as the sea is wet can't."

What was left of Nat's anger melted away as he considered his chances even before a family friend if the choice came down to him or the engineer. His shoulders slumped, and he stared at the scarred deck, a further testament to their status. No matter how much the crew scrubbed, these old boards would never shine like some of the newer ships did.

He kicked at a particularly dark spot, where dirt had embedded itself into a crack so deep it had become part of the decking and resistant to any efforts to clean it up. "I didn't eat his food." The mutter came out despite Nat's efforts to push all that away.

"I never said you did. I don't know what Mister Garth has against you, but I wouldn't have thought him sunk so deep as to make this charge. More likely he forgot it long enough for rats to polish off what they could."

"Rats."

Before the first mate could restrain him, Nat ran off to find Jenson and explain. No way would he let the cook keep thinking such lies about him, even if he accepted the truth that no good would come of a confrontation with Mister Garth.

22

G uilt as much as fear kept Sam still for a long while after the engineer, cursing the boy who'd delivered the food roundly, had stomped up the stairs and out the hatch. The ship's rocking seemed to even out, and the sounds in the room had quieted to dripping water and the creak of old wood.

She hadn't thought further than filling her belly. She hadn't meant for others to get in trouble, not when she'd left enough for him to eat. How could she have known he would question the portions? She'd even left the roll.

The food in her stomach churned in protest. Leaving the roll didn't change her decision to take the man's porridge. Just because he'd been too busy to eat and she'd been hungry wasn't reason enough to go against everything Lily had taught her.

Sam stared through the pipes at the main section, now empty of both man and food.

Everything she'd done to reach this point had caused harm, harm she'd never intended but which wouldn't have happened without her actions.

First she transformed the steam carriage though she knew she should not have. Someone could have been injured in the crash, and what the coachman would do about the damages, she had no idea. He could lose his job, or at least owe more than he could afford. Sam could hope Henry would help him, knowing the true cause, but then Henry would be the one to suffer from her actions.

Even the little boy on the dock suffered. She'd only wanted to help him find his beloved toy. Instead, she'd changed it into something monstrous in the boy's eyes—or at least his father's—costing both the train and the boy a close friend.

She remembered the look on the boy's face, but what came to mind had little to do with the train and everything to do with the mechanicals she'd imprisoned in her workshop. She'd done so for their safety, and for that of her family, but how they must be suffering. Trapped much like she'd become here in the engine room. They drew their strength from the aether so would not go hungry as she had, but to never be free, to never see her again, seemed too great a punishment. She would have been kinder to dismantle them and scatter the pieces far enough that they could not bring together enough aether to dream of their previous state.

A whimper escaped her lips though she should keep silent even now with the engineer gone to stir up trouble. If she could just learn restraint, if she could only hold back when she wanted something, or when a mechanical called out to her, then none of this would have happened. She'd still be safe back home with Lily and Henry. Lily wouldn't be so sick from worrying, and Kate might not have hated her so.

The dim interior of the engine room seemed to darken, to seep into her very being as she dwelled on all the bad choices she'd made, the myriad ways in which she'd brought trouble down on others, which only brought her back to the sailor boy.

She'd known of the engineer's vindictive nature. She'd heard enough this morning even without the sour words to the carry boy when she'd first reached for the hatch. How could she have thought taking from his bowl would pass unnoticed?

Memories of the engineer's behavior broke through her misery and made her wonder. From what she'd seen with her own eyes, the engineer would have found something wrong even had she taken none. Lily would have given her a tongue lashing if she'd ever treated one of the servants as the engineer did the sailor boy, and all when the boy had been trying to do the man a good turn. She wouldn't have put it past him to spill some of the porridge out and let it go to waste only so he could charge the boy with something.

Righteous anger drained away as she recognized this as no more than another attempt to push aside the blame. The engineer might be all she thought of him and more, but that didn't change how she'd done him a disservice as great if not greater than what he'd done to the sailor boy.

Stowing away seemed so much simpler when she'd come up with the idea—not that she'd planned for this to happen in advance. She knew too little about ships and their ways to think she could hide out safely. The best source of information she had before now was the books in Henry's library, many of which told tales as fantastical as the events that had beset her since her sister declared the time had come to cross to the Continent.

Had she any choice in the matter, she would have snuck off the same way she'd come on and gone about finding Henry's man, if for no other reason than her disappearance from the coachman's care would cause more of the very worry she'd tried to ease by leaving. Her failure only added to the many faults she had, a burden her sister had borne for too long.

Guilt and the reasons that led Sam to this place overwhelmed her until she felt them as a weight pressing her down, filling her lungs with hot, cloying air. Though her thoughts spun round and round in her head, condemning her with every turn, soon she became aware of an all-too-familiar tickle in the back of her head that grew louder than her fear.

Sam ignored it.

She couldn't let a bout take her over, not here. What would she do, what would any of them do, if she managed to transform the copper coating on the hull into something wonderful? Such a change would leave the wood to the healthy appetites of whatever insects had found their way aboard or creatures that roamed the seas in the hopes of an unprotected ship.

No matter what arguments she put forward, whether of her own making or remembered from Lily's schooling, the engine kept pressing at the back of her mind. She clung to the memories of how she had harmed others, of the suffering she left in her wake, but tendrils of desire wound through the darkest moments and shoved them aside.

At first it asked for grand changes, but she held strong.

Then it sent out feelers of aether to limn the scattered collection of gears and springs until they glowed to her eyesight. The engineer had left them to skitter across the floor as the ship moved, and some even found their way under the pipes as though to seek her out.

Sam held fast through it all, proud of her strength, until the engine begged for her help not to make it different, but to soothe the hurts brought on by a hard pounding. She'd seen the engineer's anger herself, heard the ring of his blows, and felt through the aether tendrils how his faulty efforts worsened the problem.

Surely Lily wouldn't condemn her for helping. Surely no harm could come of it.

The engine seized hold of that slight weakening and encouraged it until Sam could no longer tell which thoughts were her own and which had been inserted by the aether-driven desires.

A man like the engineer seemed the type to claim his efforts the cause rather than looking further, or at least he'd been quick enough to assign the blame to any but himself. If she fixed his fixes, why would he question?

She'd lost what shred of control had kept her back.

Sam crawled through the pipes to lay claim to the right gears and even some tools the aether highlighted for its purposes. Holding the thought that she would do repairs alone in the front of her head—no transformations, no improvements, and no wish fulfillment—she crossed the room to where the engine stood.

Her will faltered when faced with the full force of the engine's demands, but Sam whispered under her breath to remind herself. "Repair. I will only repair."

The state of the section recently worked on brought tears to Sam's eyes. She ran a finger along a particularly battered part before removing the freshly bent gear. The desire to soothe its hurts by replacing damage with something stronger, faster, swept over Sam, but she sped her whisper, her voice fierce and determined as she replaced first one gear and then the next. A spring required only shifting for its coils to smooth out, but in other areas, the tools the engineer had left proved inadequate and she bent aether to the task.

Her whole focus remained on the engine, moving over section after section, repairing the parts that had failed and others just waiting for their chance. She forgot everything else: the ship, the engineer, the risk of discovery. Nothing existed beyond the pains of this particular machine.

The only thought she clung to in the depths of her bout was the need to repair rather than change, and that with a fragile grasp.

At last, though, her supply of pilfered gears and what little energy she'd drawn from the porridge that morning ran dry.

Hands shaking, Sam backed away from the engine, longing to activate the mechanism but retaining enough sense to know what the engineer might not remember doing in his anger could cover her work, but the engine starting itself would require investigation. She gathered up the gears the engineer had used and dragged a last bit of aether forward to repair the bends from his hammer so they could be reused. Only tiny fractures, visible with aether to highlight them, remained, but she could do nothing about those.

Though exhausted, she had enough presence of mind to return his collection to the pile in case he'd yet to count them the way Cook inventoried her supplies. Besides, he'd search for an answer if she left them next to the repaired engine with the ones he'd removed as if it had ejected his brutal efforts.

Sam stumbled over the first pipe protecting her hiding spot and banged into a second, making such a clatter she expected discovery at any moment, but finally she reached what had become her home.

A pang cramped her stomach, and a groan made its way through her lips before she could stifle it, but no one had come to see what strange occurrences had taken over the engine room. The silence remained, deeper now without piteous cries coming off the engine itself.

Sam huddled around her hunger, satisfied in the thought that she'd succeeded, not just in the repair, but in controlling her bout as never before. She'd limited herself not to what the aether longed to attain but to what the mechanism needed. Though not enough to soothe her body's demands or ease her guilt at previous failures, at least considering the fact gave her some distraction from her troubles.

23

N at should have known Mister Garth would go to great lengths to make trouble, but the engineer must have shown Jenson some kind of proof to make the cook light into Nat like that. The problem bugged him through the rest of the day.

No matter what he thought of the engineer, a single burp would have given the man away had he eaten the porridge then complained. The penalties for theft were high enough, but false accusations bore a harsher penalty. Otherwise it would be too easy to use ship law to carry out grudges.

Mister Trupt, and even Phil, took Nat to task about his performance, but he couldn't bring forth the same focus and enthusiasm with this charge hanging over his head. The rest of the crew seemed to have forgotten, but he knew how easily seeds of doubt could be sown.

The captain had put off one of the rope men not more than six months before when none of the crew would trust him, and that because of a rumor following him from his previous ship rather than anything the men had seen with their own eyes.

A man's measure was in his actions, or so Jenson had claimed, but the measure could as easily be driven by the words of another, malicious or unintentional.

Nat thought he saw the reflection of that question in the barrel man when he passed the line of sailors waiting for their measure of ale, and again when the holystone for cleaning the deck slapped into his hand with more than necessary force.

All around him, the men questioned whether he had stolen, and stolen food. This soon out of port, the pantry was full, but not a one of them couldn't remember a voyage where the stores had run thin, where the wind had turned against them and the balking engine refused to carry them forth.

Even Nat, in his mere two years aboard, had experienced a time with his stomach stuck to the back of his spine, and he'd faced the question of whether the stores would give out before they spotted land.

The stories told on cold nights spoke of the worst times, of choices made that could never be mentioned in full daylight. They told of rumors chasing after the survivors as they had that unlucky crewman. Whether he'd done anything so wrong or not mattered little when a crew suspected he might if given the right conditions.

"You're a fool if you think they take the word of that man Garth over yours, boy." Mister Trupt crouched at his side as though to check his work on the deck. "Truth is we all see how the engineer treats you. But that doesn't change the facts. He's worth ten of you. Ten of almost any other man on this vessel. You keep your hands clean and don't cross him. Keep acting the way you are now, though, and you'll turn every living soul on this ship against you. Act the crook, and the crew will start to wonder if it's Garth they've misjudged."

The first mate didn't wait for a response, not that Nat could come up with one. His mind ground against the implication. Had he been acting like a thief? The way he checked every man he came across could certainly be taken that way.

He sighed at the realization. He'd done more damage to his reputation than either Jenson or Mister Garth.

Nat scrubbed harder, taking his frustrations out on the dirt ground into the wood grain as he considered his options.

He had none, to be honest.

If he stood up for himself and disputed the charge, then he'd be thrown off the ship at the next port for causing trouble with a valuable member of the crew. And if he swallowed the accusation, despite what the first mate said, he could never be sure who didn't wonder if Nat had been so selfish as to take a measure of the engineer's portion.

How could he prove something false when he didn't even know what the true charge had been? If Garth expected an overflowing plate, one brimming would still speak to some missing. Nat had left the meal as commanded. Rats could have taken their fill without Mister Garth noticing as far as he'd been from the stairs and busy at that. Without seeing the serving himself, he had no way of knowing the reason for the accusation.

He did a better job focusing on his tasks after receiving Mister Trupt's advice, but the thought of rats being at the root of his problem nibbled at the back of his mind, much as how they must have nibbled away at Mister Garth's generous serving. Everyone knew rats infested the bilge. The engine room would seem an unlikely place for them to hide. Yes, it was out of the water the pumps never quite managed to clear, but there was no source of food normally. Mister Garth wouldn't be so foolish as to store extra in there, would he? And if he was, the blame for this would fall firmly on the engineer's shoulders without Nat having to accuse.

The longer the day went on, the more that thought settled into Nat mind. A plan of sorts grew from it.

First, he had to make his apologies to Jenson. Only by helping with the biscuits could Nat get what he needed. It would be worth another shorted meal to prove his innocence and do away with any doubts the crew might harbor about him. All without confronting the engineer or causing any more trouble.

24

Never one to sit still and needing a distraction from her aching stomach, Sam fell back on the games she'd played when Lily went to work. If she could keep busy, the hunger would burn less, and the engine's whispers, softer now, would not press as much.

First she counted every pipe she could see and imagined what they might be used for. This space offered many more sights than the stable she'd spent a few months in when hiding while her sister worked at Cooper's Bakery. Memories of the bakery did not help her, though, bringing with them as they did the taste of fresh pastries along with the stench of burnt crusts. Lily could only bring those no customer would willingly buy, but Sam hadn't cared.

The smell lingered, and Sam realized it lacked the buttery undertone of burnt pastry.

She sent a careful glance at the hatch, but it remained sealed against the chance of water splashing down to interfere with the engine.

The lure of the smell, both something to think on besides her gnawing hunger and because fire in tight quarters could spell danger, drew Sam from her hiding place once again.

The pipes seemed larger, the way out to the center of the room harder, with her energy expended in fixing the engine. A small part of her grumbled that the engineer had not returned to wonder at her handiwork, but mostly she felt grateful for his continued absence.

Her glance drifted to the spot where the dish had been left unattended, and she amended her thought. She'd prefer he returned with a sumptuous meal to fill her belly, if he could do so without discovering who had taken up residence in his engine room.

Guilt stabbed once again at how quickly she thought to take his food. At least if he brought the plate, he would not blame another, but she had no right to it.

The smell drew her forward again, not food, but offering an important diversion.

Metal clanked under her foot, and Sam picked up the gears absentmindedly, threading her fingers through them and tucking them into her pockets without a second thought as she made her way across the room.

The results of her investigation proved disappointing.

The engineer had left the boiler fire burning when he still had hope he could fix the engine with his brutal tactics. The smell came from flames licking the last of the provided fuel and giving off black smoke in burning that which had nothing left to give.

Sam's hand hovered over the small pile of coal and kindling as she considered the risks in feeding the fire, but ultimately she turned away. The engineer might accept the engine repairs because he had seen to the fixing, even though her methods little resembled his, but he could not help but question a fire that burned long past when any fuel must have been exhausted.

With one last glance around the bare chamber in the hopes of finding something edible stashed in a corner, Sam withdrew once again, her growling stomach loud enough she feared the sailors above would hear her.

No one came, and with no other choice, she settled into a long wait. She brushed at a smudge on her skirt only to find something hard in her pocket, an edge of the treasure trove she'd collected. Though Sam knew she should return the gears and other bits of metal to the pile, knew the thieving increased her chances of being caught, she could not go back to contemplating her fate with nothing to keep her from worries.

In fitting her stolen parts together and testing their machining, she could forget for a moment the risks of discovery. She could push aside all thought of the dangers that awaited her in a land where she knew no one and only spoke the trade tongue. Finding the Naturals safe haven without being able to ask and while keeping her abilities hidden seemed too insurmountable a task to contemplate, especially when most considered Naturals dangerous fugitives.

When she'd set out on this journey, her focus rested on Lily and saving her sister from the stress of hiding Sam. A guided trip with assistance at every turn and people who knew who to ask and where to go seemed laughable now. How easily it should have gone. How very different the truth turned out to be.

At least she could hold onto the knowledge that Lily could not know what had happened. Even if the carriage driver had returned to tell them, surely Henry would have protected her sister from this truth. Lily had to get stronger because some day her sister and Henry would find their way to the place Sam claimed for her own and visit.

She would do whatever necessary to make sure that happened, both for her sister and for herself. After all, how difficult could it be? Henry had evidence this place existed, and she doubted whether most Naturals had a friend like him with the coin and connections to investigate so thoroughly.

Soothed both by her thoughts and the smooth touch of metal between her fingers, Sam drifted into daydreams of her gilded future, her forehead resting against the rough wooden wall of the ship, the rush of water a thin length of board from her skin.

25

"I 'll sweep up the mess in here. Happy to do it." Nat waved Jenson from the kitchen, glad to be back on the cook's good side even if it meant apologizing for something he hadn't done. The ship had too little space for grudges. Nat hadn't realized how important the crew's opinion had become to him until he thought they were all looking askance.

"You're a good kid, Nat. Just keep your hands clean from now on."

He rubbed both hands down his sleeves, knowing full well the cook had meant something much different. Still, he won a laugh. After helping with the morning biscuits, he had flour there and everywhere else. Though they tried to be careful, between unexpected jolts and the need to powder the trays so the batter didn't stick, there was enough to sweep up, enough for Nat's plan at least.

His portion sat on the shelf, braced between the wall and the lip so it wouldn't slide. Jenson had served it on his way out, leaving the porridge steaming and aromatic.

He scowled and tried not to breathe in the enticing scent.

The previous day, he'd shoveled cold porridge with no thought to taste or time to savor and been blamed for swallowing down a fresher portion. Now, if he wanted to prove his innocence, he had to give up his portion once again, not to the demands of sailing but to hungry rodents who must be infesting the engine room.

The growling of his stomach warned Nat he'd have a hard day ahead of him, but if he took a single bite, he wasn't sure he'd be able to stop.

Turning his back on the plate, he bent to the task, not just sweeping the flour clear from the counter and floor so no rats came here looking for food, but also tucking it into a length of cloth he'd borrowed for this purpose. An empty plate would prove nothing, but prints in flour could not be denied.

It seemed to take forever to clean the space, longer still because of the scents drifting over from a meal meant to be his but for which he had a bigger purpose. Finally, though, he collected the folded cloth and his plate, ready to set a trap.

Up on deck, those on watch had gathered near the prow to investigate a smudge on the horizon. Curiosity almost pulled Nat from his path. Nothing should have been there for a day or more, and the possibility of a ship, friendly or not, needed to be determined so a course could be set.

The plate in his hand reminded him of his task, and he needed to complete it quickly.

At least the distraction had pulled Mister Garth into the discussion. They may have left under full sail, but evading a pirate or an enemy privateer had little to do with pride and everything to do with survival. The engine repairs could be crucial.

Nat thought maybe his trap would prove more valuable than just clearing his name. If he revealed the rats, they could set the ship's cat in the engine room to prevent any damage from the same creatures that had taken Mister Garth's meal.

No one was paying attention to the engine hatch when he reached it. Nat lifted the wood only a small way before slipping into the shadowy interior.

His plan would fail untried if they caught him sneaking in where he didn't belong. No one would believe his intentions, not with the engineer's accusation hanging over his head. That truth almost made him give up the plan, but he could not just walk away as Mister Trupt counseled.

Nat paused long enough to let his eyes adjust to the dim space before crab-walking his way to the bottom of the step. Without moving to the floor, he reached over and placed his own meal where he'd left the engineer's the day before. This time, though, he opened his makeshift flour bag and shook it over the space around the crate until no rodent could approach the porridge without leaving a damning trail.

All he had to do now was wait, an act made more difficult by his own hunger and the steam still rising from the cooked grains. His back ached, crouched as he was on the stair, and the morning's heat had begun to filter in through the hatchway, turning his hiding spot into a hot, close space.

Time slowed and even his heart seemed to beat at a sluggish pace.

No matter how long he stayed, how still he kept, or how he fought the need to adjust his position, he heard no scrabbling. Though he ignored the greater craving to lean over and swipe just one small finger's worth of the porridge, he saw no four-footed beasts approach the plate.

What he did hear proved more troubling. Through the wood of the hatch, his name sounded not once but three times before he recognized it for the call it was in his dazed state.

Cursing under his breath, Nat abandoned his post, and his untouched meal, to seek out the first mate before Mister Trupt assumed he had shirked his responsibilities. From the irritation in the other man's voice, Nat guessed the captain needed tending.

At least no one saw him slip out of the engine room. He could pretend to have been resting under the cover of a shore boat. He'd been working with Jenson while the rest of the crew relaxed, so just maybe no one would hold it against him.

26

Sam winced at the flash of bright light when the hatch lifted, but she'd already moved past the first row of pipes before stopping to assess whether the boy had left or just let in some fresh air. No, she could not see his shadow, and if she listened carefully, his breathing no longer stirred the hot space either.

She didn't know whether he'd thought to hide from his chores or brought the engineer's breakfast without knowing the bald man had gone above. Sam didn't care.

She could see the porridge and the twist of steam still rising from it. Though she'd suffer guilt later, her shrunken stomach needed food now. She'd become vermin, and the hot porridge shouldn't go to waste.

Noises came from the deck above her, the thud of feet, bare and booted, along with muffled talk, but the hatch didn't move.

She scrambled over the remaining pipes, uncaring for how their chill made her shiver with such a reward waiting for her on the other end. She'd never felt so hungry. What little sustenance she'd gained from her portion of the first serving had gone to the engine, and more stripped from her bones as well. Nothing could keep her from the food, not thought of theft being wrong nor fear of the engineer's return.

Sam burst from hiding, ready to dive across the unprotect-ed space between her and food, then jerked to a halt so abruptly she struggled not to fall forward and leave the very prints she needed to avoid.

A fine white powder decorated the boards, fading to gray where it came across a patch of grease.

Her knees trembled, both with the effort of holding herself up and the danger she'd almost stumbled into. Whatever the cause for the powder, it had not been there before. And even if it had some purpose, like to soak up the spilled grease already discoloring the white, if she left footprints where any could see, all hope of remaining undetected would be lost.

Bad enough she consumed food meant for another, but in that she had no choice. Sailors would blame the varmints that devoured anything left unattended before they'd think of a stowaway, but not with human hand- or foot-prints telling another story.

Sam glanced toward the hatch, half expecting to see someone peering in from the outside, but it remained firmly shut.

The brighter light coming through the boards blinded her for a moment, but as soon as her vision cleared, she made her way around the powder even though it meant spending too much time out in the open for safety. If she had any idea what they'd look like, she would have tried to make a ship rat print or two, but a poor attempt would raise more questions than it answered.

She had little choice.

Staying undiscovered would mean nothing if she starved to death, and though rats could be a feast for a cat, she had no way of knowing how well they would sit in her belly, not that she'd heard or seen any so far.

The stairs creaked as she crept up the first two so she could reach through to where the dish rested on a wood crate. Though Sam flinched, that slight sound would be lost in the creaks and groans of the ship's wooden frame as it cut through the water.

She kept her attention focused on the hatch in search of the slightest motion, giving only quick glances to the plate so she could place her hands properly to snatch it up.

Once the dish rested in her possession though, Sam needed no vision to gobble the serving of porridge down, tipping the plate so she could see above the edge even as her tongue swept bites into her mouth. She gulped them down as fast as they passed the barrier of her lips, hardly taking the time to chew.

Footsteps sounded not once but twice as she ate, each time making her freeze in terror.

Still, the hatch stayed closed, and the sounds faded as quickly as they'd come.

When her tongue could find nothing more, and even a look revealed no food remaining, Sam lowered the plate back to where she'd found it. Her fear of discovery combined with extreme hunger had distracted her from the need to take only what might go unnoticed. Unlike the first time, there could be no doubt something had consumed the meal.

The trip to her hiding spot stretched her tense nerves as she had to watch for the edge of powder rather than the hatch. She'd succeeded this far, but one small slip, and she'd be brought to the captain's justice.

Sam didn't feel safe again until she lay curled, back to the sun-warmed wall. Her fingers laced through the teeth of a large gear she didn't remember collecting, but which offered her some measure of comfort. How long she had to wait before the chance to try for freedom remained unknown, and as such, it loomed endless before her. Still, she couldn't help a sense of peace with how she'd fared so far.

Fate had been with her. If only it stayed on her side for a little while longer, she'd soon find safety and happiness in a place where she would never need to hide again.

27

You!"

A hand pinched Nat's ear before he had time to react, and he struggled to keep up with the engineer in the hopes of easing the sharp pain. "I was trying to—"

"Shut your mouth. You'll tell it to the first mate and the captain. I have proof you've been sneaking in when I wasn't there."

Even had he wanted to, Nat couldn't put words together as Mister Garth increased both the pinch on Nat's earlobe and his speed. The length of the deck had never seemed so long, or so many of the crew on top at once, each staring at him a second time.

The hatch to the engine room stood open, something Nat had never seen before.

He gasped in relief when the pressure stopped, and then again when a sharp shove to the back sent him down the steps barely able to keep his footing.

There, in the open space before the piping began, stood both the captain and the first mate, as promised. Though a lantern lit the space, Nat had no inclination to look around. He glanced to the plate, and as expected, it had been licked clean.

"Look at this. It's not Jenson making free with my space, Captain. See the mess he leaves behind to taunt me? He's no use for anything and thinks he's above all of us because of a little book learning." Mister Garth paused, tugged his forelock, and added, "Begging your pardon, Captain, but you've got the title to hold our respect. He does not."

Captain Paderwatch turned to Nat, his brows lowered in as close to a frown as the man had ever worn in Nat's presence. "Is this true, Mister Bowden? Have you been plaguing the engineer and causing him trouble? I thought you had an interest in the workings. This is not the way to gain a man's consent. I thought you smarter than that."

"But I wasn't—I wouldn't—I swear—" Nat struggled to get a full sentence out in the face of the condemnation on both the senior officers' expressions.

Mister Trupt shook his head. "A man's only as good as his actions, boy. Yours don't show you well in this."

Nat ducked around the captain to grab the lamp, his passage followed by a curse from the engineer, who'd tried to catch him and failed. "I wasn't causing trouble. I was trying to prove I'd never eaten Mister Garth's share. See, the plate's proof enough. I gave up my morning meal to regain your trust. The flour will show it."

He waved the lamp over the floor, but Mister Trupt caught his arm before he could see the rat prints that were surely there.

"You stole flour too? You're not helping your case, Mister Bowden."

"I didn't do that either. Ask Jenson. I helped with the biscuits this morning even knowing I wouldn't get my share. I swept up so he could eat with the crew. It's only the waste I used. I swear."

The first mate frowned. "What did I tell you about swearing? You're too easy with the words. Makes them have little value."

"I have proof."

Captain Paderwatch intervened, putting a hand between them. "Show us this proof then, Nathaniel. You'll still stand to the charge of going where you don't belong though. You must know that."

Nat's shoulders curled, but he didn't let the statement discourage him. They needed to know he hadn't lied.

"See?" He raised the lamp high. "The flour will show signs of the rats that must have eaten Mister Garth's portion just as they ate mine. I left his by the steps as he told me to. I would never take another man's food, no matter how often he's tried to get me in trouble."

Silence fell where Nat expected agreement, the engine room growing uncomfortable.

He'd been staring at the captain and first mate. Now he turned to see the evidence.

A single boot mark showed on one side of the flour.

Beyond that, the only flaws showed dirt from the sweeping and a few clumps of dough.

Nat's hand lowered of its own accord, the flour he'd been counting on acquitting him no longer lit as the lamp fell to his side. "But the plate…"

Mister Garth let loose a harsh laugh. "He'd try anything to get out of his just punishment. This is the type of boy the Company gives us now."

Nat's fingers curled into a fist as his dislike of the engineer turned to hatred. He spun to confront the man, everything coming clear in that moment. "You did it. That boot print was from you wiping out the animal marks. You didn't want to back down on your accusation, and you're willing to cheat so you don't have to."

The engineer raised both hands as though to fend off a blow. "Hold on there, boy. I don't like your accusations."

"Now you know what it feels like, only you're guilty, and I was not."

Mister Trupt's hands came down on Nat's shoulders, holding him back though he hadn't planned to attack the man physically. He didn't need to. The others had seen the bootprint. They had to believe him.

Mister Garth's lips curled into a sneer. "And just how was I to destroy your fancy evidence as you call it? I didn't know what you were about until now, or rather what you'd like us to think you were doing here. If your hunger hadn't gotten the better of you, boy, you might just have fooled the first mate and captain into believing your story, but I've got your measure. Even if there had been rat droppings all around that plate, it doesn't explain the missing parts you took as payback for some slight you imagined. The crew might weigh the theft of food higher than any other, but the captain here knows what those gears cost. This has gone far beyond a simple prank. You get them from wherever you stashed them now, and he might go light on your sentence. But pay you will, and well."

"I didn't!" Nat started to struggle in earnest as he realized the trap the engineer had set. He'd walked right into it, having admitted to sneaking down here. "You can search my hammock and every place I've been. I didn't take anything. We wouldn't have half those parts if I hadn't gone with you to get them. I know the importance of them. I never would have taken any."

Something in the engineer's face made Nat realize he'd erred in mentioning the trip to the shipyard. Though successful beyond Mister Garth's hopes, the way the workers had treated Nat must still have grated. But the mistake had been made, and the best he could do now was to fall silent.

"So…" The engineer drew out the word as though savoring it. "You refuse to return the parts?"

Nat shook his head. "I can't return what I never took in the first place."

Mister Garth shrugged. "You heard him, gentlemen. The only other person who has been in this room is myself. I certainly wouldn't remove parts that could prove critical. He thinks to convince you of his innocence just as he denies taking my meal, but it's only pretty words. He plays on your good natures. He's just as I've always said. A troublesome boy. Why else would his fancy family have cast him out to sea on the weakest of the Company ships? You can tell from his threads they have enough to buy him a better position."

The first mate shifted his hold to Nat's upper arm and muscled them both past the gloating engineer.

As soon as they reached sunlight, Nat tried again. "You can't believe I would, Mister Trupt. I asked for this position. He's right that my parents could have given me different, but I wanted to go to sea. My mother trusts the captain to look after me. That's the truth, I sw—"

Nat choked off his words, remembering Mister Trupt's earlier caution.

The first mate pulled Nat round so he could look him in the face. "I thought I knew you, boy. You work hard, you don't complain, and you do as you're told. But we all know you've a grudge against Mister Garth. Doesn't matter whether he deserves it or no. This is serious, Mister Bowden. Not some boyish prank, but interference with the workings of the ship. If he can't get that engine running smoothly, all our lives might be at risk, not just yours. Give up your hiding spot, and the captain and I will do what we can for you."

As much as he wanted to confess, to reveal where he'd hidden the parts, Nat could only stare at his hands. He hadn't taken them, despite how it appeared. He had no idea what had happened to the parts. The thought that Mister Garth had hidden them crossed his mind, but while the engineer might be spiteful enough to run a boot through rat prints, what Nat faced now could mean hanging. Not even Mister Garth could be that cruel.

"So that's the way of it, lad? I can't say I don't understand the urge, but you're better than this. It's gone on long enough. Maybe a day or two in the gaol will make you wise. The longer you wait, the harder it'll be for you."

Nat trembled at the thought of the storeroom down in the bilge that became a jail when needed. The stench itself was enough to make a sailor regret whatever actions forced him down there, and nothing but stale bread and water were given prisoners.

"Please. I'll help search. He must have misplaced them. I can find them." He braced his foot on the doorframe the first mate had dragged him to, desperate not to enter the space.

Mister Trupt shook his head and pulled hard so Nat stumbled down the short but steep steps. "You can spare yourself this, lad. It's far too late to pretend a search. Just tell us where the parts are hidden, and you'll take your punishment in stripes instead of this and the rope that waits you now. If not for yourself, think on your mother. You're the youngest, are you not? She's sure to dote on you. Bad enough to know her son a thief. Let her not bear the weight of your death."

Nat clutched the first mate's arm, holding him where before he'd been the one held. "I swear, I do. I mean it this time more than ever before. I did not take them. I did not touch any of the parts. Mister Garth wouldn't let me. Not after what happened at the shipyard. He hates me, the man does. I didn't think he'd go this far, but I did not take anything."

The first mate pried Nat's fingers loose and gave him a firm, but gentle, shove.

Before Nat could rush forward, the door swung shut and the lock closed with a decisive thunk.

Nat pressed his ear to the thick wood, but it deadened any sound. He did not know when the first mate walked away, only that the man did not change his mind and open the door to let him free.

He sank to the floor, the stench deeper down against the heavily stained wood. He would hang for this. Unless the missing parts showed up on their own by some miracle, no hope remained for him.

28

S am stared at the patch of sunlight beaming down from the still-open hatch, half expecting the sailor to return with the boy and declare it all a mistake. He had been trying to trap her, or rather the rats he thought her to be, but he'd saved her from eating those same creatures.

Her fingers brushed the gears she'd taken, never thinking about the cost until too late. They'd just found their way into her pockets and stayed, the effort to give them back, to give up the comfort they offered, too great.

"Will these losses prevent you from fixing the engine?"

Sam froze as the well-dressed captain spoke again. She'd been so caught up in her thoughts that she'd forgotten not all of the gathering had left. The bright light made the shadows deeper, and with the lamp on the ground, they'd faded into the darkness.

"I was doing the final bits when you called out for sail," the engineer grumbled, his annoyance clear. "Any part I needed was already in place."

There was a pause, then, "And just how is it you know some parts are missing?"

"There was more when the carry boy put them here. I know it, and I'm not wrong either."

The captain coughed into his hand as though smothering a curse or calling for patience. "I expect you to take an exact inventory, Mister Garth. You've made some serious accusations. I won't have them acted upon without a full accounting of what is not here. Do you understand me?"

"Sure, sure, I'll get it done. I thought checking the repairs would be more important, but you're the captain."

The tension radiating from the captain's form was visible even in the shadows. "You're telling me you've yet to fire it up when it was done all this time?"

Footsteps moved away from both the opening and her hiding spot, heading deeper into the engine room.

The engineer grunted as he followed the captain. "Didn't want to chance tearing the sails," he said after a pause.

Sam could hear the disgust in the captain's voice when he spoke. "Well, get on with it then. The wind's been calm these past two bells. You're saying we could have been making way instead of busying the crew with shore tasks? If that smudge had turned out to be a pirate instead of an uncharted island, your patience could have cost us everything." He emphasized patience as though it were fouler than anything Henry's farmhands ever used.

Whatever the engineer replied was lost in the hiss of the boiler fire kicked into life.

Sam leaned forward, her guilt forgotten as the repairs she'd made prepared for their first-ever run. Though she'd wanted to ignite the engine as soon as she'd finished, had the engineer done the same when he had, the damage might have been more than she could fix, and certainly not without drawing notice.

Instead, gear teeth lined up perfectly as steam worked its way through the piping and drove the pistons into motion. Her nerves tingled with the aether gathering in the air as the engine grew one step stronger, better, closer to the perfection that would earn it a soul.

"Would you listen to that?"

The sound of a deep male voice broke Sam from her trance, and it took her a moment to recognize the engineer in what had been such a reverent tone.

This time the captain grunted a response.

"Goes to show you what can be done with decent parts," the engineer added, as though unsatisfied by the captain's lack of praise.

"You'd do well to remember how you came by such high-quality pieces," the captain growled, "being as you're so quick to condemn Mister Bowden."

The pipe Sam leaned against clanged as though someone had jerked into it.

"What is your meaning?"

All reverence had left the engineer's voice, and it had risen a pitch or two.

Sam crept forward in an effort to see both men, but the same pipes that protected her from their sight kept them hidden.

"Your behavior at the shipyard did not pass without notice, Mister Garth." The captain put heavy emphasis on the title. "I got the full story from a sailor I sent to see about replacing one of the torn sails. While I cannot condone his behavior, I can certainly understand what drove Mister Bowden to it. If you were half the engineer as you are a fool, you wouldn't have to worry about being stuck on a vessel with so little claim to prominence. Or perhaps it's your very foolishness that got you condemned to plague me. The boy will suffer for his response to your arrogance, and suffer harshly, but don't think I'll forget how all this came about."

The engineer wisely kept his tongue between his teeth long enough for the captain to stamp out of the engine room and slam the hatch down after him until only the faint light of the lamp remained.

Sam ignored the mutters coming from the far side of the room as the engineer pretended to check on repairs he'd been unable to make in the first place. Instead, the captain's words, meant to condemn the engineer, bit deep. She hadn't intended to cause trouble this time any more than the others. She just hadn't thought of what her actions would mean, or dismissed any consequence because the engine didn't need these gears. For the boy to suffer because of her broke everything Lily had ever taught her. Sam couldn't let it happen again.

Despite the risks with the engine room still occupied, she couldn't wait until the engineer left. He'd promised an inventory as soon as he finished with the engine. Once he counted and found the pieces gone, he'd have his proof, though against the wrong person. And how could the boy sailor ever do anything about the charge. He couldn't return what he hadn't taken.

She'd crossed this same space because of an empty belly, though that time she had reason to expect the engineer to stay busy. Now, he had nothing to do beyond delay the inventory.

Sam gathered the gears into her skirt to muffle the sound because she'd taken too many to fit in her pockets. She needed to get going before she ran out of time or nerve.

Urged on by the hiss and hum of the engine itself, she ducked between and under pipes, her movements awkward with her bundle of cloth and metal, until she crouched within reach of the pile where she'd found the parts in the first place.

She took a close look at how the bundles had been left and judged where she could tuck the pieces under a pipe. They should be found when doing inventory but might have been overlooked before because they'd slipped out of the bundle. At least they wouldn't be able to say the boy returned them, not the way they took him off under guard.

29

W hen the hatch door lifted, Sam still had a hand out with the last gear, her attention focused on the faint clunks and pings from where the engineer continued to assess her repairs.

Fear blinded her as much as the light.

If whoever opened the hatch chanced to glance down at that moment, she'd be fully visible, stretched as she was over a pipe to place the gear just so.

It fell from her numb fingers, the dull thud of metal against wood masked only because the newcomer now thumped down the first few steps to pause with the hatch half open.

She jerked back and scrambled over the next set of pipes so quickly her elbow struck one with a sharp clang.

"None of that now, you stupid old beast," the engineer cried from the back of the room.

Sam didn't know whether to be relieved he mistook her clumsiness for a problem with the engine or to sigh because he cursed the beautiful mechanism that was this ship's engine. She had time for neither, though, as she crouched down to learn why yet another had come to intrude on a space she'd thought little used.

"Better watch where you be throwing those insults."

Silence took the place of cursing as the engineer recognized he no longer commanded the space alone. Not that he ever had, but Sam wasn't about to tell him so.

"Phil? What are you doing down here pestering me?" The engineer appeared, rubbing his hands on a rag as though he'd actually been working. Sam hoped he did so for appearances alone and had not disturbed any of her changes, though he'd be unlikely to put his hands into the path of an active engine.

"Cap'n sent me to help you with an in-van-tory." He pronounced the unfamiliar word as though each syllable held a separate meaning.

The engineer glowered at this new sailor. "I'm fully capable of counting on my own."

The sailor shrugged. "Guess he thought you too busy."

"Well, you can tell him I have things well in hand."

Phil shook his head from side to side as he stepped further into the engine room and lowered the hatch to reveal he'd brought a second lamp. "I know orders when I hears them. I'm to help you, if you need me or not."

The engineer's face turned a dark enough shade that Sam could see the difference even in the dim lighting, but he offered no further protest except to bark, "Then get to gathering the pieces over there. I need to collect my manifest."

Raising his other hand to reveal a torn piece of sailcloth, Phil said, "No need. The captain sent me with what the shipyard charged for. Guess he didn't know you had one of your own."

From her vantage point, Sam saw the scowl Phil could not, but she did not know the cause. Part of her began to wonder if the engineer had, in fact, noticed the few parts she'd taken, or if he'd laid false charges after all.

"It's a waste of my time, and of yours as well," the engineer told Phil. "You'll find I'm missing a handful of gears and a couple springs. I'm not fool enough to forget what I brought back."

Sam bit her lip to stop a cry as he named just what she'd returned. It seemed he honestly believed the boy responsible for her actions. Still, she didn't know what he would do when crossed and suspected she would not like to be on the receiving end of that event.

"I only know what the Cap'n said, and that's what I'm set to do."

The engineer let out a harrumph and snatched the scrap from the sailor's hand. "Then let's get this over with. It's bad enough he takes what doesn't belong to him, but now he costs me time as well. It's just lucky my repairs are already complete."

He paused, tipping his head toward the running engine, then knelt to investigate the pile so near to Sam she ducked down in fear he'd see her, a danger that grew when the sailor joined him.

The pool of light from their combined lamps reached almost to her toes. She could not move back with them so close, either. The engineer might have dismissed the first time she bumped a pipe, but he'd been a lot farther then.

"And that accounts for this section. Only one left to check. You'll see, and so will the captain. That boy has duped the lot of you with his helpful ways. Who knows what other trouble he's been getting into."

Phil sounded as though he smothered a laugh. "The only one as has trouble with Nat is you, Mister Garth. Never been a bother up on the rigging."

"Not much room for it," the engineer answered as he sat back far enough to give Sam a glimpse of his satisfied expression. "There. Just as I said. Even accounting for the pieces currently in the engine, there are seven gears of various sizes missing, three in the larger range, and..." He tapped the list as though checking. "...two springs. Is that proof enough?"

A squeak slipped out before Sam could muffle her cry.

They hadn't found them. After her attempt to make things right, the boy would still suffer.

The engineer sneered. "And you won't convince me it's the rats, not even by making their sounds. The porridge maybe, though not with a flour trap—just proves the boy is clever— but rats have no need for gears. There's no good protecting him. It'll only go against you in the end. He doesn't consider himself as one of you, no matter how much he pretends."

Sam leaned her head on the warm metal pipe.

Once again the engineer had come up with an explanation for her foolish noises. Even if the sailor denied the charge, it wouldn't be great enough to investigate. She was safe, at the cost of the boy. At least if they looked for rats, they might chance upon the gears she'd returned.

The light shifted as the engineer moved his lamp, but Sam didn't bother to look. They were going away. She'd failed once again.

"Wait. What's that?"

Movement sounded much too close to Sam for comfort, and she chanced shifting a little deeper as she peeked at the sailor.

Whether he'd been testing the engineer, or the shift of light revealed the missing pieces with a glint of metal, the one called Phil now pulled them out one after the other.

"Not possible. That boy did this somehow. I tell you he's not to be trusted. All that book learning he had before coming here has rotted his brain."

Phil's voice dropped lower even as the engineer's rose. "How do you figure he did? Way I've seen it, he's been locked up in the bilge all this time because you didn't notice kicking some under one of these many pipes. Seems to me you owe the boy an apology."

Sam hadn't realized how much taller the lanky sailor stood than the engineer until then.

The engineer sputtered. "An apology? He planted the gears here. He must have. I swear they weren't there before."

Phil shook his head back and forth slowly. "What is it Mister Trupt always says about giving your word so light?"

Sam could feel the air in the room heat as the engineer's eyes narrowed. "You. You put them there just to make a fool of me. You like the boy. You always have. And now you think saving him from the consequences of his actions is doing him a good turn. It's not. It never is. You do them good and all they learn is how to grow up even more trouble."

The moment he got his last word out, the sailor attacked. Sam barely saw him move, but Phil had the engineer by the scruff of the neck like a misbehaving pup.

"First you accuse Nat. Now you accuse me. Shut that mouth, or I'll think you kicked the pieces aside on purpose and will tell the captain exactly that. As it is, we're taking the results to him right now."

For the first time since he'd come down, the sailor did not shorten the captain's title, nor was his tone as laid back as it had been.

A flash of sympathy for the engineer startled her, but not enough to regret the sailor's quick thinking. Only she knew the true cause for the missing gears, but as quick as the engineer had been to cast blame, she knew who the real troublemaker was.

"You can't do this. I'm the engineer. You're nothing but a rope rat. Let me go."

The protests faded only by distance and the thud of the hatch closing. Sam didn't think it likely the engineer would meekly submit once they'd achieved open air, though perhaps the sailor loosened his hold to dim the man's arguments.

All pleasure at the engineer's condition faded as she realized two lamps remained in the space, shedding light where she'd only seen glimpses before. She could pick one up and explore every facet of the room without chancing the danger of calling aether to this already rich area as a way to highlight the metal.

As tempting as the thought of exploring might be, what else the two men had left captured her attention more fiercely.

The sailor's lamp set her gears and springs agleam with an enticing sheen of metal cut or stamped into function. They'd already done the count. After being made a fool of before the crew, dragged about like a child, the engineer would hesitate to claim missing parts a second time.

Her whole body cried to move forward, to sweep up pieces her hands already knew the shape and feel of, but Sam pulled back instead. She couldn't free her gaze, but with distance, the demand lessened and she could breathe a little easier.

Sam huddled in her corner, trying to understand what had happened. She'd never found such a pull from simple parts. They could not draw enough aether to trigger her bouts, or so she'd always thought. Either she'd grown stronger away from Lily's calming influence, or the engine enlivened everything about it.

30

Nat scratched a dirty finger against the pitted wood, unable to see the black under his nail, or even the wood making the walls of his cell.

Down here where the bells did not penetrate over the hum and hiss of the engine, where sunlight had not touched since the ribs of this hull stood bare as the one in the shipyard, every minute seemed like an hour, or every hour like a minute.

He had no idea how long he'd been locked below. They might not bother to feed him. Why waste supplies when the charge held a penalty of hanging? From the stench, he could only guess at the privy though that could just be the bilge.

Nat tried playing games in his head, going over the math tables his tutor had tried to drum into him despite the slim odds that he'd ever be in a place to use them.

He tried telling himself they'd figure out he hadn't stolen the parts. That they'd set him free and toss the engineer in here in his place, but the pitch dark of his cell mocked any such hopes.

The captain had his word alone against that of the engineer—a valuable member of the crew, especially with such a faulty engine. And he had snuck into the engine room, with the best of intentions, but he didn't need the first mate's caution to know he should have left well enough alone. If only he'd listened to Mister Trupt. Better he'd been cast overboard in the last storm they'd weathered than this.

"Ware your eyes."

The door swung open so close on the warning Nat barely managed to throw an arm in front of his face before bright light filled the tiny room, illuminating every encrusted inch.

Nat blinked hard to wash away tears he pretended were caused by the flash of light instead of what would come next.

His vision cleared to reveal Phil rather than Mister Trupt who he'd been expecting. Nat cried out a greeting, clinging to the sailor's unexpected presence, but Phil stepped to one side to reveal not just Mister Trupt, but the captain and engineer as well.

His shoulders slumped as he understood what had happened. They'd tried one more search and failed to find the pieces. Since he could not do as Mister Trupt commanded and tell them where they could find what they believed he'd taken, they must have decided he'd cast the gears overboard. At least they did not plan to leave him to starve while they returned to port.

He pushed to his feet, determined to have these last moments speak well of him. His eyes watered a second time, with no handy excuse, at the thought of his poor mother receiving the news, but he refused to acknowledge the chill trails they left down his cheeks.

Mister Trupt pushed forward and took hold of Nat's upper arm with a surprisingly gentle touch. He must have seen the defeat in Nat's posture, because he left off more questions Nat could not answer. He just marched Nat from the cell and up the steps into sunlight many times more brilliant than the lamp had been.

Though the silent procession unnerved him, Nat felt grateful at the same time not to be forced to keep his composure as men he'd thought of as friends now walked him to the hangman's noose. He could hear the others coming up behind them and drove himself forward though he could barely see. He didn't want them to run into his back or be left to stand on the steps as Mister Trupt had to drag Nat onward.

At least the light kept him from seeing their destination. As long as the noose remained hidden from view, he would be able to maintain his firm countenance. He had nothing else left to him and could not change the outcome either. In this slight measure, though, he would do his mother proud.

"That's far enough, Mister Trupt."

The captain's voice sounded sterner than Nat had ever heard it, but never had he been scolded for something so serious. Swallowing down a final, worthless plea, Nat glanced around for the rope he would wear. He needed this over with before he made a fool of himself.

"Mister Garth, while it seemed appropriate for you to deliver your words in the filth and darkness, Mister Bowden deserved better. Speak your piece in full where all can hear."

Nat straightened his back and opened his eyes as wide as he could so the wind dried them. Whatever the engineer's latest charge, it made no difference. Nothing could be worse than what he already faced.

Where Nat expected a gloating expression, the engineer looked quite grim. Maybe he had not thought his accusations would go this far.

"Mister Garth?"

The warning in the captain's tone confused Nat, as did the sharp shove Phil gave to one who should have been considered his superior.

The engineer coughed hard enough to seem as though he were choking, an impression solidified by the first words from his mouth. "I apologize."

"Mister Garth." Again Captain Paderwatch wasted no words but let his ominous tone carry the meaning.

Nat glanced at the captain, confusion now clear on his face, he felt sure, for all to see.

The slam of a boot against the deck as the engineer stumbled forward jerked Nat's attention back to the man who had been his undoing but now seemed undone.

Mister Garth glared over his shoulder at Phil, but did not protest. Instead, he faced forward and straightened his back much as Nat had done, his gaze over Nat's left shoulder. "I apologize for my accusations regarding the engine parts. When I did an inventory—"

"When we did," interjected Phil.

"When I did an inventory assisted by this sailor, we found the missing pieces. They had fallen beneath one of the pipes and out of sight, most likely dropped by that clumsy carry boy."

The first mate growled wordlessly, and Mister Garth raised both hands in surrender. "It matters not. You didn't take critical parts. You did go where you should not have, and the question of the porridge remains unresolved, but—"

Again he jerked forward, shoved so hard Nat had to catch him or the engineer would have fallen to the deck.

Mister Garth pulled away without a word of thanks and took two steps toward the nearby engine room hatch.

"And..."

The engineer jerked up like one of those marionettes at the market, as though his strings were pulled taut.

"Must I?" he appealed to the captain.

Captain Paderwatch lowered his chin in a slow nod, and all the strength went out of the engineer, leaving Mister Garth much smaller than before.

"And to make it up to you for this error, you will be allowed full access to the engine room." The words came out sharp and slow, dragged against the man's will.

A cough from the first mate made Mister Garth sink even lower, though Nat wouldn't have thought it possible.

The engineer gave a long sigh before adding, "And you'll be working with me."

Nat didn't understand at first.

His mind still reeled over the thought that, instead of hanging, he'd won access to the engine room, something no one else on the ship had besides the officers and Garth.

Then those last words sank in.

He didn't know whether to cheer or pass out from the unexpected nature, but before he could do either, the captain closed a firm hand on his shoulder and caught the engineer with the other.

"This isn't a gift for anyone. It's a responsibility. This is my ship, and I won't have petty fights aboard it. I'd hate to see either of you left on the dock at our next landing. This is your opportunity to see beyond your differences and learn to work together."

Nat took the captain's words to heart, hearing more than just what he said. Any gloating or pressure on his part would cost him more almost than the engineer's accusations. Innocence could only be lost once, and he'd just regained his.

"Aye, aye, Captain," Mister Garth said, the effort to keep his tone level obvious. "Can we get back to work now? There's much to do."

The even sounds from the engine, smoother than Nat had ever heard them before, made the statement into a lie. Still, no one questioned it, especially not Nat. He followed quietly behind the engineer, determined to win this man over.

And with legitimate access, he felt sure he could put an end to any last doubts and solve the mystery of the porridge. Though Mister Trupt said it would be forgotten, Mister Garth clearly had not done so any more than Nat had.

31

"I've finished greasing the gears, Mister Garth. What would you like me to do next?"

Sam watched from the shadows as she had for two days now. She thought she saw the beginnings of respect growing in the engineer's expression and heard it in his voice. Though he continued to be grumpy about sharing the space, Nat's willingness to do even the most grueling of tasks would win over anyone. Twice the man had seemed on the verge of giving a gruff word of encouragement before he stifled the urge.

She half feared Nat would be sent among the pipes to dust them, but if the engineer had plans for that task, he must be waiting for them to get to shore, because neither ventured into the maze of metal tubes she'd made her home.

"Did you see any rat droppings down there?"

What might have been teasing in another tone came out as a rough growl. The engineer made sure to remind Nat of his attempt to trap her several times every day, perhaps not warming to the boy as much as she'd believed.

The reminder had an effect on her as well, making her stomach ache with renewed force at the absence of sustenance.

She leaned forward, half hoping he'd say he had so she could seek them out, the idea of gnawing on raw rat meat no longer so unappealing.

The engineer stared at Nat for a moment as though expecting the boy to explode into anger.

Nat gave a weak laugh though his shoulders curled. "There's been no food. They must have moved on to richer pastures."

When he got no more reaction than that, Mister Garth scowled. "They better have. If a storm comes in, and I have to work the day and night through, there better be no reduction of my food."

Nat turned away, his face clear to Sam as he muttered, "I hope not," low enough she could only make out the meaning from the shape of his lips.

If she had half his patience and ability to endure, she would never need to worry about her gift again. She could keep her hands still and away from all the mechanisms that called to her.

As though awake to any shift in her thoughts, the engine sent out feelers, ready for its next transformation and having gathered enough aether from the atmosphere to call out again.

This time, she had little difficulty ignoring its cries. Not only did the engineer rarely leave his space unwatched, even taking to sleeping at the base of the steps, but many days on little food followed by these last few with none had left her too weak to do more than observe.

The aether tried to pull her in, but she had no energy for it to claim. This control came out of weakness, one she would gladly dispense with given any opportunity even though gaining command of her gift could win her safe passage to the haven.

Where she'd expected Nat to keep trying to catch her, instead he made sure no food stuffs lay unattended in the engine room, even carrying the engineer's meal to him on the one occasion where Mister Garth kept working. Sam didn't know what he did back there, the engine itself not visible from any of the safe paths she'd discovered, but at least he did not undo her repairs.

Her only hope now lay in them reaching the Continent before they discovered her refuge, or before starvation drove her from hiding. She'd milked brackish water from the pipes using a steam release valve, most of the salt left behind in the process, so she stood no danger of dying from thirst, but the layer of fat Cook had cultivated with every meal had melted away until her thick bones lay close against her skin.

Even had food been plentiful, the effort she'd put into the engine would have stripped her form. As it was, she could not renew what she needed, and each attempt by the aether to capture her took a little more of what she could ill afford to lose.

"Have you found any that could be spares?"

She forced her attention back to Nat and Mister Garth, their interactions all that kept her from curling into a corner and losing herself in the pangs of hunger.

"They all seem pretty worn. And some of the teeth are bent. Maybe the shipyard back in Dover could repair them?"

"Not even your friends there can do much once the teeth are gone. It's melting and recasting for these. It's a wonder the steam engine held together at all. At least now it's keeping on."

That was the closest Sam ever heard the engineer come to recognizing Nat's involvement in getting the better parts, something she'd learned from overhearing earlier discussions. She had much to thank the boy for beyond just food. The engineer might not be the best at maintaining his engine, but he'd spoken the truth about the gears he'd identified as too flawed to continue. She'd seen the state of them in the pile he'd left by the engine. Those gears had lost what value they must once have had and had been destroying the very engine they were supposed to enable.

With its new parts, the engine hummed along without stopping, and each day her repairs gave hope they'd reach the port sooner than if they'd gone under sail alone. She only needed to hold on a little longer, or so Sam told herself. The ship would have to stop in for supplies even if it traversed the length of the Mediterranean before finding its proper landing. Once they reached a port, she'd surely be able to find food and a direction.

She had to believe in that truth else she'd go mad of hunger if the nibbles on her consciousness begging her for energy she could not supply didn't drive her there first.

32

N at sometimes thought he saw a glimmer of respect in the engineer's expression, and Mister Garth had muttered a few half-hearted compliments, but still Nat had no time alone in the engine room. And with Mister Garth bringing up the porridge at every turn, he knew the engineer continued to believe he'd taken the food because of a grudge.

Neither had the question of the missing food left Nat's mind, though he'd been unable to do much of anything about it. Mister Garth might tease about the absence of rat droppings, but Nat had been searching for just such a sign and finding nothing. His only hope lay in setting another, better, trap. Which meant the engineer had to leave the space long enough to overcome the instincts of whatever beast—rat, cat, or maybe even dog—had stolen aboard the ship and hidden in the unlikely spot of the engine room. The beast, if still here, must have been starving by this point.

He lay in his hammock at night thinking over just how his dusting for prints had failed and had realized two weak points. He'd dusted the flour across the floor, but hadn't been able to stay long enough to see the animal, which meant the steps were free for use by whatever had eaten the food. The sailors might see rats as nothing more than a nuisance, but they freely admitted the little creatures had enough thought to know when a ship had been damaged beyond repair. Rats may have had enough sense to recognize the flour as too risky a pathway.

"Mister Bowden. A word."

Nat froze at the first mate's call, his arms tense around the sack of coal he carried to restock the boiler. Though he'd done everything asked of him, and caused no more disruption, he couldn't help remembering what had happened so few days before. He wondered how long it would be before he could relax back into his old role. Mister Garth holding the question of the food over him made such a state impossible no matter how much common sense—and Mister Trupt—told him to leave it be.

The first mate strode over to him, unhindered by the boat's rocking. Wind slammed them with waves towering almost higher than the deck, too rough for the sheets, which had all been furled. Only the engine kept them moving, its paddlewheels striking below the turbulent waters, protected from the same with wooden shielding.

"Yes, sir?" Nat kept his gaze down and his stance respectful.

"The captain has called a dinner this evening to recognize the work Mister Garth has done in fixing the engine. It's never run so smooth."

Nat bit back a sigh. He'd collected the old gears for the engineer. The ones he'd earned were made from a metal with twice the strength and a cleaner cut, but Mister Garth would happily take the credit. "I'll tell him to make ready." He turned to continue toward the engine hatch.

"Not so quickly, young Bowden. He means to honor you as well. Maybe not for the quirk that gained you the shipyard's approval…" The first mate raised an eyebrow to show Nat had failed to cover his reaction. "But he has found your behavior since the incident exemplary. A lesser man would have balked at being asked to work with the very sailor that almost cost him his life. And no one ever said Garth was easy to work with on the best of days. So, yes, go tell Mister Garth, but ready yourself as well."

"Yes, sir." His response held more enthusiasm and his step on the way rose a little higher, but by the time Nat reached the hatch, he could have kicked himself for showing any sign of discontent. Not that he thought Mister Trupt would report his moment of weakness. It was more that he'd realized how opportunity had slipped through his fingers.

With Mister Garth at the captain's table, he'd have had long enough to entice out the starving creature or creatures that haunted the engine room. He'd finally be able to wipe away any lingering doubts from the minds of the engineer and the rest of the crew. Whether the captain had intended to include him, or Mister Trupt made the change in recognition of some truth to Nat's honest reaction, there would be no way to avoid such an invitation now.

"The captain's table, eh?" Mister Garth said as soon as Nat passed the message. His face split into a satisfied grin.

It took less than a heartbeat for the engineer to see the other side to it, though. "You thinking of coming here, then?" he added as if able to read Nat's mind.

Nat shook his head. "I have been called as well."

That soured the engineer's mood, but he gathered himself enough to say, "A mighty big honor the captain's table. Not like when you eat with him in his cabin, boy. It's a formal meal, though I suppose you've seen your share of those at your fancy home. Still, you'll need to be on your best behavior. Show us both up fine."

"I will." Nat brushed past the engineer with his load, trying to ignore the fluttering that started in his stomach from the combination of missing the first, and possibly last, chance to catch the creature along with the pressure to live up to the captain's mealtime expectations without further alienating Mister Garth with his "fancy ways."

Once they landed, anything smart enough to avoid his trap would most likely take advantage of the confusion to slip off the vessel, or at least to an area where food seemed more abundant. If Nat had any hope of removing this taint, he needed to come up with an explanation for the missing food, proof that did not involve him.

As to the dinner itself, despite what Mister Trupt said were the captain's intentions, if he made any mention of the quality of parts, or if Nat's childhood table manners far outshone those of the engineer, he could offend the very man whose nature had already proved sensitive to such things.

The hours between Mister Trupt's invitation and the dinner bell both raced and crawled. Each minute offered more distraction and further upset to his stomach until Nat shivered with the force of it. Never had he felt more vulnerable, not even when he believed himself on a march to the noose.

At least then the answer had already been given. Here, he navigated a stretch with rocks on one side and too short a draw on the other. A single misstep could lead to disaster.

"Time to go splash some water over your face and hands, Mister Bowden. Wouldn't want to disgrace yourself in coming to the table."

Mister Garth seemed almost fatherly as he escorted Nat up the stairs and into the evening light, but he was in no condition to appreciate the normally sour engineer's jovial moment. He stumbled on the last step and only stopped his face from meeting the recently swabbed deck with both hands. Pain raced up his elbows from his wrists, adding to his dizzy head.

"Are you feeling all right? You don't look so good." The engineer pulled Nat back to his feet.

He swayed there, a movement that threatened to cause another tumble as the waves sent the deck counter to his motion.

Mister Garth caught his upper arm in a tight grip that had little to do with anger. "Boy, you're the color of shallow water over algae. It's not a good sign."

Nat swallowed hard. "I'll be fine," he managed, his words slow and labored even in such a short phrase.

The engineer shook his head. "You will not. Something in Jenson's cooking looks to have sat poorly in your gut. I'll make your excuses to the captain. There's no way you'll be any good at his table." Without waiting for a response, he waved another sailor over. "Escort this young man to his hammock and see he stays there. I need him healthy, not vomiting all over the engine."

"No problem, Mister Garth."

Nat glanced over to see Garth had chosen Phil as his escort. Already, the thought of avoiding the treacherous ground at the captain's table had eased some of the pressure on his head and stomach. Not enough, though, for him to protest as the sailor supported him back to his hammock. His head still spun and his stomach churned, making a quiet rest sound appealing.

"I'll leave you here, Nat, but I'll be back soon with a dry apple and hardtack. It's a sailor's remedy. Sure to ease the rough waters in your gut. Lie down and rest, if you can."

True to his word, Phil returned with the food, but Nat pretended to be asleep. Sailor's remedy or not, he had no intention of putting anything in his stomach. He had a feeling it would taste little better going down than it would on the return journey, and he had no hope of even a single bite choosing to stay.

Phil tucked a cloth bundle of food next to Nat in his hammock so no rats would come and eat this as well. Nat heard the sailor make his way back to the deck and his own meal, one that would last a much shorter time than the formal dinner Mister Garth now suffered through. The engineer, though, might find both the attention and higher quality of food on the captain's table worth the effort, even if most of the sailors would have rejected the fare.

Captain Paderwatch rarely called together more than a couple of his officers, and even more rarely included Mister Garth among them. An honor indeed, and one Nat felt grateful he'd managed to avoid.

Still, sleep eluded him. Though his stomach pain eased, he did not feel up to partaking of the meager collection Phil considered a cure for what ailed him. Nat had never been one to suffer from stress before.

He felt so tentative now in the face of what had happened and what could happen again at the least excuse. Maybe not a hanging, but Captain Paderwatch made it clear friendly feelings and old favors only stretched so far. If Nat slipped up a second time, he'd be put off at the nearest dock with little hope of a recommendation to find himself another berth.

So much balanced on the slender point of Mister Garth's acceptance.

He could not change who he was, or what he'd been. He could only prove to the engineer that he expected nothing for that past, nothing more than the chance to establish himself. And he already had a black mark against him in this endeavor, one he did not deserve.

33

Sounds from above settled as the crew found places on the open deck to eat. If the wind were too strong or the rain falling, they'd come to eat here, among the hammocks. Only the captain had a sheltered place to eat for every mealtime.

Nat envisioned the deck, each group finding their normal spots with him floating among them, friend of all but bound to none.

He dug for the apple Phil had left for him though he hadn't consciously recognized the first twinges of hunger. Nat brought the dried fruit to his lips, but paused before taking a bite. The mental vision of the deck above moved to take in the empty space in front of the engine hatch where Mister Garth chose to camp when he wasn't up on the bow with the spot within clear view.

His fingers tensed hard enough to bruise a fruit still ripe with juice, though the apple in his hand hardly matched that description.

He had everything he needed in the food from Phil and the empty watch spot. Nat could finally do something about his situation.

The cramps in his stomach, whether left over from his earlier pains or brought anew by hunger, didn't matter when weighed against a chance to clear his name, one that might never come again.

Both legs went over the edge, and he made a shaky dismount, but his head no longer spun, at least not with vertigo. Instead, his thoughts worked out a plan that could not fail—it must not. This time he'd place the trap at the very edge of the pipes and would not leave for anything.

The creature or creatures would think themselves safely hidden under the pipes, while Mister Garth would be busy at the dinner. Nat had no doubt jokes about his absent sea legs were already passing among the crew, part in warning about a sickness and part because Phil couldn't keep an amusing tale to himself. No one would expect him to be up and about.

He could not have found a better circumstance had he engineered it on purpose.

The dark offered a cloak about his shoulders as he made his way across the space between the crew hatch and that of the engine room. Knowing where everyone chose to eat, Nat had only to look for strays, disgruntled sailors or those who had offended enough to be cast aside for the day or so it took to get over whatever made them separate.

He ducked around a shadow that could have been coiled ropes or a sulking crewman, and waited for a cloud to diffuse the moon's light before scrambling to the engine hatch, his path only slightly hindered by the weakness that persisted in his knees. He held a doused lantern in one hand and the bundle of food in the other. Falling would have made him look even more the fool.

Another cloud gave him the time he needed to duck inside, while a roar of laughter from one group of sailors masked any noise he might have made.

Nat stumbled down the steps, almost dropping the lantern when he went from impeded vision to pitch black. The bundle with the food fell from his other hand as he used that appendage to brace against impact. His food vanished into the gloom.

He hadn't considered just how dark the engine room would be without either sunlight coming through the cracks or a lamp to light his way.

His breathing sounded overly loud along with the echoes of his thudding entrance, but though he hung there frozen for longer than comfortable, no one came to investigate. It seemed he'd arrived in the engine room without detection, as much by the grace of fate as his own clumsy planning.

While he'd waited for an alarm to sound, his eyes had adjusted to the room well enough to make out the banked fire that kept the boiler going during the night. Not willing to chance the ship meeting an obstacle too small or dark to be seen in time, the captain had Mister Garth lower the flames to smoldering so the boiler did not cool but neither did it push the paddles round fast enough to drive them into the unknown before the lookout could call and the steersman react.

Here his plan held solid.

Making his way across the dark chamber afforded Nat more than a dozen bruises from pipes and levers he'd never consciously noticed in the lit room, an uncomfortable journey. Still, when he reached the fire, its glow revealed the kindling he'd added to the supply just that afternoon. A quick bit of prodding, and he had a spill to light his lantern.

Nat released a sigh of relief as the shielded lantern revealed more of the space where he stood and turned an unfamiliar territory into one well known from all his labors.

As the sound of his sigh faded, though, he heard a different noise, something that didn't belong in a space populated only by the low-set boiler's barely audible hum.

The scrape of rough sackcloth against the deck.

He closed his fist, only to remember how the cloth-bound food fell from his grasp on the steps. His idea for a trap was working all too well, but with him too far to catch sight of the villain much less apprehend the creature to prove he would never steal another man's food.

Nat stalked toward the steps, fighting the instinct to run. He had to keep quiet or the creatures would scatter.

There must be more than one rat, or something the size of a dog, to drag the bundle so quickly. And smarter than he'd thought. Whatever haunted the engine room could not help but be starving, and yet had not torn open the bundle and began to feed right there.

If he hadn't been listening to the emotion in his sigh, Nat wondered if he'd have noticed the faint dragging sound in time.

As he turned the corner, Nat raised the shield to fill the room with brilliant light, at least compared to the darkness of a moment before. He'd kept the flame within his vision so he wouldn't be blinded, but the squeak from his quarry showed it had no such protection.

A flash of movement and a clatter of pipes gave Nat a direction.

He set off in pursuit, the lantern showing him a path through the maze so small that even with the aid of sight, he made enough noise to bring the whole crew down on him, or so it seemed.

Still, the creature moved faster, always just beyond his vision, making a clear sight of its shape impossible. Doubts about the wisdom of chasing after a desperate beast whose manner he knew not crept into Nat's head while his body kept pushing forward, but the curve of the ship's outer wall showed before he could hesitate.

He had it cornered.

Nat raised the lantern high, wanting to see what he'd caught up with before crawling through the last set of pipes to a space too small to give either of them room to maneuver.

34

S am pressed her back against the rough wall, unable to go any further. Her feet scrabbled on the deck as though trying to push her through the wooden planks, but nothing could stop the light from reaching her.

She watched, fascinated, terrified, as a pale yellow wash came closer and closer, seeming to take forever though she knew time had slowed like tree sap in the winter, trapping her in the instant before she lost everything.

The light crossed her toes and rose higher before it paused as she heard a gasp.

She tore her gaze from the yellow and squinted beyond it to see none other than the boy, Nat. He'd caught her after all.

She'd harmed him time and again without ever meaning to. Of all those to discover her, it had to be him.

Pleas dried in her throat, only a cracked whisper of nonsense making it past the gate of her lips. Exhaustion, hunger, and fear stole any bit of language, leaving only the certainty he'd be happy to see her tossed overboard, thrown into the water without even a plank to float on.

The boy stared back, seemingly as speechless as she found herself. Or maybe he contemplated all the ways he could exact revenge, how he would make her pay for every moment she'd cost him.

He blinked twice then shook his head as though just coming awake.

She drew in a breath, waiting for the shout that would bring the rest running.

Instead, the pool of light shifted as he turned back the way he'd come.

Sam stayed frozen, unable to understand his intentions. In the back of her mind, a voice screamed to run, to burrow deeper into the pipes and engine until no one could find her. She could transform the engine, change it to become a suit of armor, a place of safety where none could disturb her. She could transform the ship itself, using the pipes stretched throughout its form as pathways for the aether necessary to bring it to life.

She did nothing except shudder as the light returned, bobbing with the boy's motions. He twisted through the pipes, sometimes over, sometimes under, but never away.

He had found her in this place, and he would find her again. She could feel the determination radiating off him as though he too had drawn aether from the air.

Without him, she would have starved.

Without her, he would still hold whatever privileges her interference had cost him.

They were bound together.

35

The path through the pipes seemed as clear as day with the open lantern. He couldn't believe it had taken him so long to notice a girl. How could she have stayed hidden here, have taken food he'd brought not once but twice, and he'd never caught even a glimpse of her?

The laugh building in his chest threatened to become a hysterical giggle as Nat considered all the scenarios he'd imagined. He never could have come up with something like this.

She'd looked so young and scared, cowering away from him as though he'd landed a blow on her skin rather than simple lamp light. How she came to be there, he couldn't guess, but she was too far from home at this point to make for an easy return no matter what her circumstances.

At last, the light fell on the bundle he sought, its absence from her hands telling him she'd dropped it in the scramble. Nat swept it up and headed back to her hiding place, half expecting the girl to have vanished, or maybe transformed into a mangy dog with sharp teeth, the vision a consequence of his sickness.

But no, a young girl with a pale face still cowered against the ship's wall as though frozen.

This time, he leaned over the last pipe to set the lantern on the floor. He needed his hands free to untie the bundle.

Again, she stared at him with the whites showing all around her eyes. Her body shivered without stopping despite the warmth filling the chamber from even a banked fire.

"It's okay. Don't be scared. I won't hurt you."

He wondered if she even spoke the English tongue. He hadn't understood a word coming from her mouth earlier, but her face changed, her eyes narrowing and her brows drawing together as though puzzled.

Nat glanced away long enough to untangle a knot grown tight in their chase.

He heard more than saw her move, his body going tense in expectation of the need to catch her once again.

Instead, she'd drawn her knees up under her and sat much like the dog he'd expected her to be. Her head tilted to one side as she watched him.

The realization brought forth an odd thought.

He wondered how much she'd watched him before. Did she know his disgrace, and how close he'd come to having his neck stretched out over the water?

His fingers continued working at the knot though his thoughts had wandered, and it gave way when he was not ready.

The apple came free to drop to the ground with a thwack. It started to roll under the pipe separating them.

Momentum carried the apple toward the girl. She lowered a hand to stop the fruit from going any further then lifted it up.

He waited for her to bite the desiccated fruit and tear some free. She must have been starved if the last time she'd eaten was when he'd tried to trap her with his porridge.

The girl looked at it for long enough he wanted to say it wasn't poisoned or foul, but before he could speak, she held her hand out, the untouched apple on her palm.

Nat shook his head. "It's for you. Eat it." In case she couldn't understand, he motioned lifting a sphere to his lips and biting into it.

The gesture was enough to awaken his own hunger, and his stomach growled its anger at the decision to cast food away.

The girl jerked her hand toward him again, but he refused.

She put the apple on the floor as far from her as she could reach without moving.

Nat climbed over the last barrier, finding the space tighter than he'd expected as the pipe cut off the curve of the hull. He squeezed into the farthest corner and crossed his legs under him, trying to remove any appearance of threat.

The apple sat between them, slightly closer to him.

As much as his stomach demanded he accept her refusal, he could guess how long it had been since she'd seen a meal from how tight the skin on her cheeks had stretched.

She sank back onto her haunches, but did not settle, her posture one that could result in an explosion of speed he would never be able to match, folded as he was.

Somehow, Nat didn't think she had it in her to run again.

His rumbling stomach had been full that noon. Hers had last seen a portion of porridge several days before. The trembling hadn't stop even now, and he wondered how much was fear, and how much due to a body used past exhaustion with nothing but itself to consume.

Nat nudged the apple closer to her.

The girl didn't move.

His gaze fell on the bundle, discarded in the confrontation over the apple.

He could just reach it.

Nat pulled the cloth under the pipe until he could lift the hardtack from within its folds. He tapped it against the floor to dislodge any mealworms before setting the bread beside the apple and waving toward her.

"You eat it. I had porridge for breakfast and stew for lunch to keep my strength up. Jenson will give me a meal even now if I go to him."

She still hesitated, but when he gestured again, she dove on the food, cramming both into her mouth at the same time and choking.

Nat unwound himself faster than he'd have thought possible as he grabbed the food away.

She gave him a wounded look and shrank back into her corner.

"No—"

She flinched before he could finish his sentence.

He put out a hand with the apple in his palm. "It's yours. Just, you have to go slower. If you don't choke, you'll make yourself sick. Slowly."

The girl reached out and snatched the apple, but this time she gnawed on it, tearing off strips of the dry flesh and staring at him as she chewed methodically before swallowing.

Nat settled again, closer now, and waited for her to tire of the apple before offering the bread. She seemed much like the feral dogs that roamed the docks, fed by all and none, kicked by many.

If he had anything to say about it, she'd be kept safe until she lost that look of fear and the pinch of hunger. She reminded him of his little sister though this girl had reddish hair rather than black curls. The urge to protect her made any other thought of little consequence.

36

Sam kept her attention focused on the boy even as she tore into the food he'd given her. After the trouble she'd brought him, this generosity made her nervous. When he'd leapt at her, she'd expected violence, not rescue.

She didn't understand him at all.

He did nothing more, not talking or moving except to relieve the pressure in his legs, but she knew he'd react quickly enough if she tried to waste his gift.

The aged apple and hard bread made her throat dry, but her stomach welcomed the food even more for its ability to sit heavy without bloating. She drew out the process, at first because of his warning, and then because she didn't know what to do next.

She owed him something, both for the food and not calling the others when he discovered her presence.

He could not be ignorant of her involvement in his problems. He'd set traps to catch her already. So why did he feed her? Why keep her secret?

His lips curved in a tentative smile, and Sam felt her face responding in kind despite her questions.

She ducked her head only to catch sight of her now ragged skirt, and the smears of dirt and porridge on her hands.

No, he could have no questions about her.

Sam drew her legs under her, only then remembering she'd removed her boots some time ago and he'd been staring at her bare toes. She must appear no better than a ragamuffin, a child of the streets much like that policeman thought.

Her shoulders slumped, his opinion carrying weight though it should not, but how could this be any worse than when she revealed the truth. His kindness most likely meant he had not tied her to the missing gears, that he accepted the belief they'd been kicked out of sight rather than stolen and returned.

As much as Sam wanted to pretend he wouldn't care about her nature any more than Henry did, she'd seen what she could have done written in aether when terror took over. Had she possessed only a fraction less control, or had not been starving, this vessel would no longer be afloat.

They might appreciate her work on the engine, much more than the coachman she'd startled, but only because they did not know the source. And she could not deny their fears. Not when she'd laid the groundwork for transforming their whole measure of security in this vast water into a device purposed solely for her own protection for all she had not acted on it.

Sam stared at the edge of her skirt, the last bit of hardtack turning to crumbs in her restless fingers. She could only imagine how many times a Natural bout had sunk a ship before the sailors started comparing notes and determined the cause, the risk, in carrying a Natural. She could almost understand the pressure to lock Naturals away if these were the dangers she posed. Crashing a carriage seemed a minor fault compared to drowning the whole crew.

"Do you really want to waste that?"

She jerked her head up, too caught by her worries to remember his presence. He couldn't know. And she couldn't be the one to tell him, her only ally on this vessel.

The crumbs had collected on her dirty skirt. She made a point of picking up each and every one to show she had no intention of wasting this gift or any other.

"Can you talk?" He flushed. "I mean English. Can you understand me?"

A giggle escaped her before she could stop it. A ragamuffin? No, more like some feral child who had been raised by street dogs.

"Yes."

His eyes widened at her use of the formal term, and Sam realized her language would give her away. She might not have been raised by the nobility, but they'd been with Henry long enough to have picked up his speech patterns, and Sam hadn't been a street urchin to begin with.

She blushed, heat radiating up her neck. "I kin," she tried in as good an imitation of the dock voices she'd overheard as she could manage.

Nat lowered his chin in a slow nod. "A foreigner then?"

Her efforts must not have been as successful as she'd hoped, but he offered a way out, an excuse for blunders rising from her isolated upbringing and mangled attempts to fit in. Sam owed him for feeding her, and for how he'd borne the consequences of her actions, but maybe he didn't need the whole truth. Maybe she could give him enough truth to make him happy without telling him the one thing that would risk it all.

Better to be caught a stowaway than revealed to be a Natural. Maybe they'd make her work for her passage, or maybe he'd find enough sympathy to let her stay hidden.

"You don't have to answer my questions if it troubles you."

She'd stayed silent too long, calculating what to say next. Half wild, half mute, and touched in the head on top of it. She wondered why he didn't run screaming.

"I kin answer. No trouble. Me parents, they sent me to a convent, but carriage crashed."

Her broken words seemed to satisfy him where her silence had not. The Natural haven seemed a convent of sorts where she'd be cloistered with others of her kind, and Henry and Lily had been her parents in all but birth, especially Lily.

"Why stow away, though? Surely the captain would have honored your passage. This holds more dangers than the starvation you've already suffered."

She hoped he forgave her hesitation as language rather than what it was. How could she explain why she'd gone from a carriage to running ragged on the docks? She'd already thrown away any chance of being the ragamuffin she appeared without realizing it. Her story of carriages and convents drawn from Henry's books had little to do with a street child's life.

"Oh," Nat said, rubbing his forehead as though it pained him. "The crash. You must have been injured, or the coachman. What of your escort?"

Sam raised her arms in the same type of shrug she'd seen Henry's Continental friends use when she peered down through the bannister instead of keeping hidden. The boy seemed perfectly capable and willing to fill in any holes in her story, meaning fewer lies she'd have to tell and remember.

"The captain will help you. He's a good man and far traveled. He might even speak your language so you don't have to struggle."

She didn't need to pretend as she shrank back against the rough wood. "Please. Please don't tell anyone. Just let me hide here until we reach a port. From there I can make my way. I swear I'll be no trouble."

Nat paused in the act of reaching for her.

She could tell he'd noticed her failure to maintain the broken English she'd used to create her story.

He settled back on his heels and stared at her. "I said you didn't have to explain. You didn't have to lie."

Tears flooded Sam's eyes, but she blinked them back, unwilling to show such a weakness. "I'm afraid," she whispered, giving him some of the truth he wanted. "I need to get to the Continent, and I missed my ship because of the carriage crash. I didn't lie about that."

Where she'd expected anger, Nat laughed. "But you weren't quick to correct me when I made my own assumptions. Fair enough. I can't just leave you here though. People will notice if I bring food, and I won't let you starve."

Sam shook her head. "No more. You've done enough. I'll last. Just forget you ever saw me."

37

Nat stared at her before he glanced down at his hands, work hardened and little like the soft scholar's skin he'd once had.

She lied to him even now, and had lied from the very start. He'd be a fool not to turn her in. Stowing away was a crime, one bearing the same punishment as theft, and for the same reason. Supplies were tight, especially when weather or equipment could change how long even a simple voyage took, and they were on no simple jaunt to the Continent as she'd supposed.

He completed the thought, but knew he'd keep her secret.

He couldn't send her to the noose he'd narrowly avoided, not when he looked in her eyes and saw his little sister. Why ever she hid, whatever put a cultured girl into the engine room of the Company's weakest vessel in a ragged skirt with hands caked in filth, this had to be more than a schoolgirl prank.

Any able-bodied man was found work in a productive trade. With rare exceptions, though, upper class women retained their traditional roles with the focus being maintaining a home and finding a good husband.

Much of her story rang true. And he remembered hearing of a spectacular carriage crash not far from the docks. None of the gossip had mentioned a female passenger or her companion, but the chance of two such events occurring so close together seemed unlikely.

Nat opened his mouth to ask why her parents thought it best for her to be cloistered, but at the last moment, he regained his wits and remembered his manners. "I don't know what brought you to this state, but you wouldn't have come lightly. A stowaway is no better than a thief in the crew's eyes, in the Company's too. You've suffered too much to come to that end."

Color returned to skin that had bleached white as she tried to blend into the rough boards behind her. She relaxed enough to lower her body to the floor. "So you'll leave me here?"

"How can I? If you deserve no hanging, you don't deserve this either."

She reached out a hand toward him but stopped short of touching his calloused fingers. "There is no other choice. I swear. I'll be quiet. No one will know I'm here."

Nat's lips curved. "You shouldn't be so loose with your word," he said, parroting the first mate's favorite phrase.

Her whole body tensed. "I meant it. No more stealing food…no more anything. Just give me the chance to get free."

"The captain's different. He'll recognize you for what you are—"

His reassurance choked off in the face of her terrified expression, eyes wide and hands white around the knuckles under a layer of dirt.

"Please." She thrust up onto her knees as though in the very cloister she'd been heading for. "Please don't tell him. Especially not him. Please."

All thought of turning this problem over to the captain's more capable hands vanished in the face of her reaction. Nat moved forward to pull her into a reassuring hug without thinking.

Though he'd thought the space too small, she squeezed between the nearest set of pipes to an even smaller place where three crossed over, so desperate to escape his touch that she trapped herself more thoroughly than before.

"Hush, hush," he whispered as though gentling a wild-eyed foal. "The captain's a good man, and he's traveled the world so he knows the kind of things to drive a man…or girl…to desperate measures. He'd help you more than I ever can, but I won't tell him if you really don't want me to. You can stay here. I'll find a way to bring you food."

She pinched her lips tight together and shook her head violently, rejecting the idea of telling the captain, he knew, not his offer of food.

Nat settled back to watch her face, all he could see through the space between pipes. "Okay, no captain and no crew. I'll bring you something to eat whenever I can, and when we reach port, I'll help you get to where you were supposed to be going. You'll stay here and be quiet until then so no one finds you, especially not Mister Garth."

The sound of the engineer's name brought the consequences of his choice to the fore. If he kept to this agreement, he could never clear his name. Mister Garth would go on believing he'd been the one to steal the porridge, and that he'd attempted to cover up his crime by the ruse of trying to catch the true culprit.

"Thank you."

Her whispered response cut through his doubts and made it clear which choice he wanted to make, and which he should. His name, no matter how wrongly tarnished, wasn't worth her life.

"Can you tell me what to call you, at least? So I know what to say when I come down. So you'll know it's me who has come with food?"

Her smile showed teeth too well cared for to deny her upbringing even had she kept to the broken speech. At least merchant, if not full on nobility, would be his guess.

Something inside Nat awoke at that realization. He hadn't realized how much he'd missed the chance to converse with someone who likely knew the same things he'd known, someone who didn't hold his future hostage the way the captain did, whether he meant to or not.

"I am Samantha. Sam."

Lost in his wonder at finding a companion when, even before the other sailors started doubting him, Nat had not found a place to belong, he almost missed her announcement. But when he did hear it, the short boy's name seemed too intimate, too rough for a sheltered girl bound for a cloister despite the fate life had thrust upon her.

"Well, Miss Samantha, it's very nice to meet you. I'm Nat...Nathaniel Bowden."

As though they were back in his mother's drawing room, two young people amid a gathering of greybeards, she held out her hand for him to take, threading it between the pipes that still kept her captive.

Nat bent his head and pressed his lips to the back of a hand almost as rough as his own. His mouth curved against her skin at the incongruity, but she deserved proper treatment when she must see all this as a nightmare from which she could never wake.

Samantha giggled and withdrew her hand to give him a hesitant look.

Nat returned her gaze with a full grin only to freeze as something in the changing sounds above warned him the men had gone back to work.

"I can't stay. If I'm caught, you'll be found, or I'll be hung for interfering with the engine, neither of which are what I want, nor should you. I'll be back though. I promise I'll come as soon as I can manage. You'll know it's me when I call out to you. If you don't hear your name, whatever you do, stay hidden."

He waited long enough to see her nod of agreement, though he supposed he hadn't needed to warn her considering how well she'd done through the first part of their voyage. Still, warmth settled into his chest at the thought of his secret friend waiting for him, trusting him. Nothing, not even the thought of suffering Mister Garth's pokes in silence, could dampen that knowledge.

38

S am watched him go, the warmth of his friendship strengthening her as much as the food he'd shared though his own stomach rumbled with desire for it. Since the carriage crashed, leaving her abandoned among strangers who would only do her harm, she had yet to feel safe.

Now she did.

She couldn't imagine what she'd done to deserve this, how fate could have led Nat to her side instead of another sailor, or worse Mister Garth, who would condemn her out of hand. For him, more than any of the others, she would keep under control until they reached their destination. She would not risk her only friend no matter what the engine offered her.

Just the thought of having Nat to talk to when he could take that chance made the engine's whispers less enticing.

Sam hugged her legs and stared out through the pipes, anticipating when next he would come. Even watching him work with the engineer when he could do nothing to acknowledge her presence would be comforting. She no longer felt as alone as she had when no one knew she was there.

She only wished she could tell him the whole truth, but how could she ask him to go against everything he'd been told? Henry had, but he'd come to know her as a person first before he had to consider whether she could be the monster English laws declared her.

Nat had seen nothing of her beyond acts that would have brought the strongest of scolding's down on her head. She couldn't chance his reaction. Already, he chose to help her when by ship's law she'd most likely be condemned. She refused to add to the burden she'd laid on his shoulders, though not by intention.

If she kept her wits about her, and focused on whatever moments he could spare to visit, he would never need to know more. They could part as friends when the journey reached its end and she'd become a pleasant memory instead of a nightmare.

39

Whether from the undefinable pleasure of knowing something Mister Garth did not, or finally coming to terms with his inability to change the crew's mind, Nat walked taller the next day. He held his shoulders back and found grins came easy for the first time since being accused of theft.

Nat remembered something his mother had said as he watched the change in how the crew treated him now that he no longer curried their favor while expecting to be kicked.

His father had fought against those coming to absorb him into the new definition of industry when Nat was a young boy. He'd come back battered and bruised.

His mother held Nat through the tears, waiting until after they stopped to tell him, "If you act like a victim, those around you will treat you like one. If you act strong, they'll recognize your strength."

Despite his beatings, Nat's father had been one of the few in the nobility to enter this new age with a job that meant something. Most held figurehead positions like the captain's for all that Professor Paderwatch had turned out to be uniquely suited to the task.

He'd never fully understood her meaning until now.

Even Mister Garth seemed changed, though that came as much from being invited to the captain's table as anything Nat had done.

"You're looking a might bit better today, Mister Bowden. You missed a good spread at the captain's table with your weak innards."

Nat shrugged as he swung down the steps to the engine room, forcing himself not to glance around for Samantha.

Mister Garth stared at him for a moment with his shaggy eyebrows lowered, then the engineer shrugged too. "I don't know what's getting into you, boy, but seems to me some of that baby fat's gone missing."

With the engineer's back turned, Nat allowed himself a smile. Unless he missed his guess, Mister Garth had just suggested he'd become a man, or closer to it.

"Stop looking for those invisible rats and get yourself over here. We've got some parts to grease down really well today."

Nat's smile vanished as he stared after the engineer, stunned more at the gentle teasing in the man's tone than bothered by the words. If he'd known the best way to win Mister Garth's respect was by refusing to flinch from the probing reminders, he'd have been much faster to give up protesting.

The real reason for his change in attitude peered out from between two pipes, her grin wide enough for the both of them.

"Well, are you coming, boy?"

Nat made himself shake his head and wave her back into hiding as he strode to where Mister Garth settled in to work.

The last sounded more like the engineer he knew, but he didn't let the return weaken his mood.

His step felt lighter for having seen Samantha and having shared the unexpected softening, no matter how brief, in the engineer's dislike.

He'd mourn when she left the ship for good, but he intended to enjoy every bit of time in her presence he could manage, and with the way the engineer had acted, freedom to come and go from this space just might not be as far off as he had thought.

Thank You for Reading

Thank you for reading *Secrets*, the first of The Steamship Chronicles. I hope you have enjoyed it. The series will follow Sam and Nat as they face danger and adventure in pursuit of their hopes and dreams. Their story is just beginning.

I love to hear about your experiences with my characters, so drop me a line in email to:

* author@margaretmcgaffeyfisk.com

or use the contact form on:

* margaretmcgaffeyfisk.com

And while you are there, if you sign up for my monthly newsletter, I'll share a bit of my writing and publishing journey, fun events, and even snippets or pre-publication stories as a thank you for letting me into your inbox. You can also choose to receive release announcements, which are split into genre and go out only when a new book is available in that genre. Feel free to select as many options as you'd like.

Finally, can I ask a favor? If you're willing, I'd appreciate a review of *Secrets*. Your feedback will help The Steamship Chronicles find the right audience. If you choose to review on your website as well as retail and/or reader sites, you can also send me the link with permission to include it on that book's information page, if you're so inclined.

If you'd like to read excerpts from *Threats*, Book Two of The Steamship Chronicles, and *Safe Haven*, the story of how Henry and Lily met, please turn the page.

Threats

Book Two of The Steamship Chronicles

"Samantha?" Nat's whisper sounded overly loud with the engine shut down, but he didn't know how much time he had before Mister Garth returned from relieving himself over the side. A few days before, the engineer would never have considered letting Nat stay down there alone for even so short a time, and that was a trust he didn't want to lose. "Samantha?"

An icy chill raced down his spine when she didn't answer his repeated call.

The biscuit he'd saved from breakfast seemed little enough to sustain a body. He'd tried his best to save something from every meal, but he hadn't managed each time. Nor had it always been possible to give what he'd reserved to her without arousing the engineer's suspicions.

Nat glanced toward the hatch, closed against the inclement weather, and slid between the copper pipes. He could always claim to have heard the hiss of steam escaping. Mister Garth had him wrap a weakened section just yesterday, the pipes old and worn as much as the rest of their vessel.

But she had a good heart and a good crew. He wouldn't choose to be on any other ship in the Company's fleet.

"Have you food?"

Nat slammed his head into a pipe, his reaction threatening to cause the very damage he'd hoped to use for an excuse. His teeth closed down over his tongue to hold back words his mother would have whipped him for speaking in the presence of a lady, no matter how threadbare and dirty her clothes.

"Not much for you, but it's what I was able to secret away."

How she managed to traverse the pipes with little more than a whisper of cloth he had no idea. She made him feel twice his size and more in the fashion of a bumbling circus bear than a man full grown.

She rubbed the back of one hand over her eyes, offering a hint as to her delayed response. "I have no right to complain. You've done so much for me, more than most others would have."

A wide grin spread across his face, and he ducked to hide the reaction to her praise. "It was nothing. No more than any decent fellow might do."

Out of the corner of his eye, he saw her shake her head, a movement that sent her lank hair to swaying, offering a hint of its beauty when properly tended. Sure, she had coal dust smeared across one cheek and grease under chipped nails, but Nat could sense she'd clean up right fine. Too fine for the likes of him no matter what his family had been, at least until he earned command of his own steamship.

"Can I have it?"

The hint of laughter in her voice made a wave of heat rush up from under his collar. Grateful for the dimly lit space, he dug out the biscuit. At the same time, he marveled over her change in demeanor now that she had food, irregular as her meals might be. He would never have mistaken her for a street child now.

Samantha took the biscuit from his hand and nibbled it slowly, requiring no reminder to make it last unlike the first time he'd offered her food in amongst the pipes. She no longer seemed feral, though he could not imagine any of the young ladies who'd made his acquaintance in his mother's drawing room managing these circumstances half so fair.

He lingered though he knew he should get back to the task of cleaning coal dust and soot from the valves, in this, a rare break from running the engine. Mister Garth had been almost as reluctant as the captain to shut it down, not wanting to end such a long run without trouble. Still, if the pipes clogged or the gears bound, they'd be back to where they'd been before, or maybe worse if the engine shook itself apart.

Nat twisted in the tight space, knowing his duty for all that Samantha fascinated him.

She stopped eating and brushed her fingers along his arm, enough to get his attention without restraining him.

Another young girl might have begged him to stay, desperate for the company, but Samantha had not shown that kind of weakness. If the isolation pained her, she would never sink him with the knowledge.

"I must be getting back. Mister Garth could return any moment."

"I don't mean to keep you," she said, her voice softer even than a whisper. "It's just I'd thought the trip to the Continent a short one. When will we make land?"

Nat sank to his heels, his body twined around the pipes in an uncomfortable fashion as he twisted back to look at her. His tongue felt heavy as his mind raced forward. He'd forgotten his decision not to burden her with where they were truly headed when he first learned of her existence. She couldn't have changed anything. By now, though, he'd thought she'd have figured it out.

"You still think we're bound to the Continent."

Her shoulders rose. "Where else?"

Between one heartbeat and the next, she went from self-sufficient and amazingly strong to a sheltered girl with no understanding of the ways of trade or sea passage.

A sigh rustled past Nat's lips. "If we'd been heading for the Continent, we wouldn't have been more than a day or so before the first port. Even those steaming up the Med stop in France or Spain to offload the post and the occasional passenger. It'll be a long time before you fetch up on those shores."

The darkness that shadowed her blue eyes told him her question had not been as much out of ignorance as he'd thought. He wished more than anything to wash her fears away. "Have you no one in the colonies?"

She shook her head, her jaw tightening in the way he'd grown used to seeing when she set her mind to something even with their short acquaintance. "None I know of." She sucked in a breath. "I'll manage. I've gotten this far."

Her reaction startled a laugh out of him. "You'll go much farther before we're done. Don't worry. Captain Paderwatch has a good head for the trades, and he gives us each a share of the earnings once his costs are repaid. I should net enough to buy you passage back home, or on to the Continent, once we reach land."

"You've done so much."

He didn't have the chance to reply because the steady clomp of boot heels approaching thudded overhead, an affectation the engineer maintained even when anyone beyond the officers went barefoot.

After a quick wave goodbye, he turned and started winding through the pipes to get into place, leaving Samantha to her limited repast and even slimmer hopes.

He should have told her, if not when she'd first revealed the misunderstanding, then any number of times since. How had he failed to consider the impact of each day passing as her belief in their destination slowly crumbled? Her strength might have been born of the understanding that her ordeal would soon end, something she could no longer hold on to.

Their passage would be measured in weeks. The runs across the Channel took a fraction of that time.

He'd survive on short rations, but she'd suffer more than he would, especially with little hope of giving her anything other than stew-soaked bread. Even without the difficulty of the dishes, he had no way to hold back his porridge or stew without raising the very suspicions they both needed to avoid.

Nat slipped back amongst the soot-darkened valves and picked up his rag just in time.

The hatch swung open, and Mister Garth stomped his way down to the chamber.

Though he bent to his task, Nat's thoughts spun a familiar revolution. He questioned, as he had many times before, the wisdom of giving in to her pleas not to tell the captain back when they'd been no more than a few days out. The consequences to their schedule if they'd turned back then were not to be considered, but how could he have let her become the very rats he'd suspected her of being, living in hiding with only crumbs to sustain her.

Despite her fears, the captain was a good man.

Nat sighed. Whatever he thought now, he could not reveal her without making his involvement obvious.

"Don't be so glum, Mister Bowden. It might be dirty work, but it's important. Think back on when you woulda done anything to get permission to come through that hatch. You got what you'd wished for."

Mister Garth gave a laugh that held a gruff edge but none of the bitterness Nat had first faced from the engineer. He'd gone a long way toward proving his worth to the man, and nothing would convince him to give up the gains.

Not that he'd been frowning over the task, anyway. If the engineer thought it grimier than scrubbing down the deck boards, he'd been too long below.

Nat let the teasing pass without comment, more so he wouldn't be pushed to explain the true source of his upset than out of any need to suffer it.

The way Samantha's predicament gnawed at his mind, he'd be hard pressed not to fail both her and himself in blurting out his concerns. He had no right to share them with anyone, certainly not the self-same man who, a short time ago, was willing to see Nat hang on the suspicion of theft. How much more harshly would Garth deal with one who'd stowed away?

Purchase a copy at your
local bookstore or preferred online vendor.

Excerpt

Safe Haven

Prequel to The Steamship Chronicles

Eight years before Secrets, *Lily and Sam were hiding in London as they hoped to find passage to the Continent. Instead, they found Henry.*

S o, Madam, can you describe the mechanical?"

Henry Stapleton tapped his charcoal stick against a piece of paper, keeping the notebook angled away from the housekeeper. He'd learned, when he first joined the police force, where his uniform might not win him answers, the appearance of writing would.

After all, the staff had been trained for generations to bow before nobility, and only the upper class could write.

The housekeeper wrung her hands so strongly he feared she'd strip the flesh from her bones. "He'll blame us, Sir. I swear none of the staff put a hand on the cursed thing. Only brings the attention of Naturals, it does, having those contraptions in the house."

She leaned in close to add, "He thinks it makes 'im big. Important like. He goes showing it off to everyone. No wonder it's gone missing." She glanced around, features pinched as though worried she'd been overheard.

Henry swallowed a sigh. He'd joined the police force to help people in need, not track down rich men's toys. Some family legacy he followed. Though if it took the edge of fear from this woman and the rest of her staff, at least he'd have accomplished something.

Their master should be whipped for how he clearly treated those in his employ, but it wouldn't happen. The laws had yet to catch up to this new world where blacksmiths could put out steam-driven mechanicals and the new industry raised country merchants to the big houses. His father would have rejoiced to see this come about in his lifetime, if he'd lived, without noticing the troubles it brought.

"Don't you worry, Madam. We'll find your master's mechanical, and who's behind this rash of thefts."

"Thank you, Officer Henry. Thank you." She grabbed his hand and clutched it between her pillow breasts. "I can't tell you how much safer we feel with you about."

"Just doing my job." Henry extracted the hand and touched the rim of his top hat in a half salute. "I'd best get back to my team."

He'd gained a reputation as the voice for the small folk despite his bloodline, but hearing her, a soul would think he did so much more than take their word as evidence. His grandfather had hidden political fugitives. His father helped bring about laws to protect the weak. Just listening seemed too little an action to win such approval.

He turned away before his frustration caused him to lash out at the one who didn't deserve it, but she caught hold of his arm and pulled him back.

"You said a rash of thefts, Officer Henry. You don't think…" Her fingers tightened even more as she failed to bring forth the rest of the question.

A short laugh escaped before Henry could corral it. "Mum, we haven't seen a Natural on the loose in over a year, and never down here in these parts. Mechanical contraptions are expensive. Those that have them tend to wave the devices about just asking for them to be lifted. You said so yourself. More like some enterprising fellow is taking them up on the challenge and reselling the mechanicals for a steep profit."

She released him with a laugh of her own, one hand pressed to her bosom. "Oh, Officer Henry, I'm sure you have the right of it. The stories one hears are enough to send terror through the stoutest of hearts, but not yours. No sir, not Officer Henry. I'll keep you no longer. You'll find the fellow and bring him to justice for all of us."

"My team and I will have this wrapped up in no time," he said, squashing the inappropriate hope that this time it would be something more than just a common thief. He strode down the steps to join the other officers where they'd gathered in the street.

Catching a Natural would make a difference to more than just the wealthy. Naturals posed a real danger to the people with their wild contraptions running about harming folks. He'd seen them in the asylum—all new officers were required to do a stint there. Pale, wraith-like beings only vaguely showing their human beginnings.

That stint was the first time he'd left his grandfather's pocket watch behind since he inherited it. No metal objects of any kind were allowed within, but one of the attendants had been kind—or cruel—enough to demonstrate the reason behind the rule. Memory of those grasping hands and mewling cries haunted his dreams for weeks afterward.

"So, Sergeant, what you think it is this time?" Fitz asked, his words thick with the Irish brogue he'd shown no signs of losing.

Henry shrugged. "What else? A bunch of wealthy men showing off their contraptions to any comer." He glanced from one to the other of his five men, settling at last on Parson, a Scot from upcountry. "Tell me any of you found something more interesting."

They each waved their own notebooks, filled with random marks because none could read or write beyond their names, but those they interviewed never knew the difference.

"You know I can no more read those scratches than tea leaves." Henry said with a laugh. "Ken, what do your instincts tell you?"

Nicknamed for his ability to sense the truth behind almost anything, the skinny man looked nothing like a police officer, but Ken had better instincts than any other Henry had seen. Other officers had tried to pull him to their teams, but he'd refused each time, something that brought Henry a measure of relief.

Tugging on his forelock as though the night-dark strands held the meaning of the universe, Ken stared at the ground while his mind churned through the possibilities.

The others waited patiently despite the chill of late fall. Better patience now than wasting time Ken could have saved them.

Henry stamped his feet and wound his scarf tighter around his neck.

"Sergeant, it doesn't make sense. Not so many. What thief is so skilled, and yet so foolish, as to keep coming back to the same place?"

Ken's words brought a tension to every one of the six of them, the implications what an officer longed for—and dreaded.

Henry's heart beat faster. Here he could make a difference on par at least in part with that of his ancestry. Only a matter of time before the Natural started building mechanical monsters to terrorize everyone regardless of social position. The monsters got their name from a natural affinity to all things mechanical while their nature could not have been further from the meaning of that word.

ILY SMOOTHED AWAY THE WRINKLES from where her fingers had clenched on her best skirt.

The solicitor continued his list of her father's debts, unaware of how his words condemned her, and condemned her sister Samantha most of all.

Mr. Cooper, Lily's employer and a friend of the family, shot her a concerned look, but she forced a smile on her face and tried to listen.

The solicitor paused to draw in a breath, his sunken eyes blinking at her and Mr. Cooper as though just becoming aware of their presence. "Now it's not as bad as all that," he said, rubbing his temple with one hand. "You have a good job and a place to stay thanks to Mr. Cooper here. I know it's not what you'd hoped, especially with having to sell your family home, but it's not like you'll be sent to debtors' prison."

Lily just sat frozen with her hands once again tangled in the rich fabric she'd never be able to replace, not here nor on the Continent where they'd been planning to go.

"Lily, you're a hard worker, don't think I haven't noticed in all these years you've been working at my bakery." Mr. Cooper sent her a kindly smile, a fatherly one when she had no father left. "I should have done this sooner, but there was the age to consider what with you being younger than some, and I didn't know what you'd planned once your inheritance cleared."

He paused, and the solicitor waved a hand as though to encourage him to go on.

They thought they had it all figured out. That the promotion Mr. Cooper had hinted at for a year now, even when her father still breathed, would solve all her problems.

"It's about time I spend less of the day at the bakery anyway, or so my housekeeper, Edna, tells me. I'll put you in charge of the place, with a reasonable increase in your pay, of course."

The solicitor clasped his hands together and grinned a little too enthusiastically, showing he hadn't been as immune to the impact of his accounting as she'd thought. "So it's all settled then. And a pretty girl like you from a respectable background, and with a good job, well, you should soon find a husband to care for you so you're not out on your own."

Lily rose, yards of cloth falling into place to hide her trembling knees. "Thank you, both of you. I'm sure I'll do just fine. I'd best get back to the bakery."

She was happy to hear the firm tone she used on the youngest of bakery girls issue from her lips. They meant well, but she could not take their kindness any more, not when they knew nothing of her sister, or rather both thought Sam had died at a young age. It had been the only way to protect her, but Lily never expected to face this alone. Her father had been healthy and strong despite all the troubles life sent his way.

Mr. Cooper laughed once. "As you see, she's already been in charge, and we all know it. I should have promoted you long ago, but never expected..."

His face turned the color it did when pulling hot bread from the oven, and his words stopped.

Lily put out a hand to brush his arm lightly. "I know you didn't, Mr. Cooper. None of us did. But you've been such a help in these past six months since Father died, even before that truth be told. He couldn't have chosen a better friend."

She swallowed hard against the threat of tears. She couldn't afford to give in to her grief, not now, and not ever. All their plans to take Sam to the Continent, to one of the few places she would be safe, destroyed in a single, horrifying moment. If only her father hadn't gone to Dover on business that morning. If only the carriage had held true. If only he'd been more frugal.

None of that could be changed now, so it didn't matter. She had to be strong for her sister. She had to figure out some way to fix this. They'd been counting on the inheritance, especially once it became clear hiding Sam at her lodgings was too risky. The abandoned stables Lily had found would not be comfortable once the winter's grip took hold, but now it would have to serve until the passenger ships started running again in the spring.

"He was a good man," Mr. Cooper said, clearly not for the first time. "We shall all miss him."

Lily stifled a bark of laughter, knowing it would take her too close to hysteria and be something she could never explain to these two gentlemen. A good man for sure, and a better father than any others knew. These two would have had him clapped in chains for the choices he'd made, her along with him.

"Come, Lily. Let's not dwell on what we can't change. There's baked goods to be tending." Mr. Cooper tucked her hand around his arm and turned to the door, his determined cheerfulness one of the things she'd always liked about her father's friend, a bright light in the gloom that threatened to swallow her family whole.

"Wait," the solicitor cried, "there's more."

Lily shivered, her body unable to mask the upset a moment longer.

"No, no." The solicitor rounded his desk, arms waving as though to wipe her fear away. "Don't you worry. Nothing bad. The debts are paid."

She focused on that fact with all her might, pushing aside the awareness that besides the single trunk of clothes she'd been allowed to take, everything else was gone. Every memento of her mother, every bit of inheritance from her father, the paintings, carpets, and statuettes that had decorated their home, all sold at auction. Even the toys she and Sam used to play with were gone, vanished just like both parents: one in childbirth and the other to a carriage accident.

"It's just I almost forgot what with all the bad news today. Your father had a single request about his belongings in the unlikely event of his early death. He asked that his journals be saved for you. They have only sentimental value I'm sure, not that I pried into his personal thoughts mind you, but they would have fetched nothing at auction."

He kept on about how little value the journals had, but his words became a blur as she tried to comprehend what he was saying.

Not until he placed the seven leather-bound diaries into her hands did she accept what he gave her. Tears sprung unbidden to fall on the top edges as she clutched this tangible piece of her beloved father to her. A sharp image of her father bent over these very books to record his thoughts came to her, a vision she'd seen every night as far back as she could remember. Within these pages, she'd find her father's voice restored to her and to Sam so they could keep his memory fresh and know him better even than when he still lived.

"There now, no need to fall to pieces."

The solicitor, when she raised watery eyes to look upon him, seemed flustered and actually backed away from her.

This time Lily did laugh, a small hiccup of sound as her lips spread into the first genuine smile since entering his tidy office. "Thank you for these. It means so much to have something to remember him by."

The man nodded twice, enthusiasm replacing a fearful expression. "Glad I could give you something. Sorry it couldn't be more, but what with his debts…"

Lily waved off further words with just her fingers, unwilling to chance dropping her father's journals. "No need. I understand better than you know. Thank you again for his words."

She spun for the door once again, but now her steps had more eagerness than weight. For the first time since her father's death, she felt close to him instead of abandoned.

About the Author

Margaret McGaffey Fisk is a story-teller who explores tales across genres and worlds. Raised in the Foreign Service where she developed a love for anthropology, she has been a data entry clerk, veterinary tech, editor, support engineer, and programmer, among other roles. She pulls on her studies and experiences to give depth to the cultures and people that form the heart of her stories. As her website is titled, she offers tales to tide you over.

She'd love to hear from you through any of the contact points or social media accounts listed on her website, or you can subscribe to one of her newsletters for release announcements, snippets, and other news:

margaretmcgaffeyfisk.com/subscribe-to-my-newsletter/

Website
MargaretMcGaffeyFisk.com

Acknowledgements

I'd like to thank David Bridger for encouraging me to write this story after hearing the barest idea and making sure it never fell off the table until he got the chance to read *Secrets*.

My husband Colin deserves thanks as always for supporting my publishing by proofreading my novels and performing numerous other tasks. *Secrets* also benefitted from the critical eye of my son Jacob. While other family members offered cover feedback, special thanks goes to my little sister, Deirdre, who contributed her face to make Samantha come alive. Erin Hartshorn also had an important hand in putting together the marketing text that most likely led you to check out *Secrets*.

I'd also like to thank Blue Harvest Creative for the lovely imprint logo they designed for me.

As you can see, though I'm taking this indie journey, I am not walking it alone. The last piece of my publishing process, and the last essential group, is you, my readers. Thank you for allowing me to bend your figurative ear and for welcoming my characters into your lives.

www.ingramcontent.com/pod-product-compliance
Lightning Source LLC
Chambersburg PA
CBHW030625120726
47904CB00006B/2039

* 9 7 8 1 6 3 1 3 9 0 0 5 0 *